The
Maladjusted

The
Maladjusted

Derek Hayes

thistledown press

Thistledown Press Ltd.
118 - 20th Street West
Saskatoon, Saskatchewan, S7M 0W6
www.thistledownpress.com

Library and Archives Canada Cataloguing in Publication

Hayes, Derek, 1969-
The maladjusted / Derek Hayes.

Short stories.
ISBN 978-1-897235-90-4

I. Title.
PS8615.A8385M34 2011   C813'.6   C2011-905350-0

Cover and book design by Jackie Forrie
Printed and bound in Canada

Thistledown Press gratefully acknowledges the financial assistance of the Canada Council for the Arts, the Saskatchewan Arts Board, and the Government of Canada through the Canada Book Fund for its publishing program.

ACKNOWLEDGEMENTS

Thanks to Rob Galikowski, Jon Millard, Ramona Sattaur, Kelly Hayes, Tim Hayes, Lily Tse and members of my writing group for reading earlier versions of these stories.

I am grateful to Ed Zile, David Drouin and Lauretta Hayes for reading them and providing suggestions. I'd especially like to thank Daniel Garber for reading each story thoroughly three times, for his editing and for giving me helpful feedback along the way. Finally, I owe thanks to Michael Kenyon for his editing and keen eye, and to Thistledown Press.

For Lauretta Hayes and in memory of Doug Hayes

CONTENTS

A FEEL FOR AMERICA

WE'RE WAITING FOR MR. HOU, THE OWNER of our school and this building, to arrive. Adam's striking a soccer ball with his right foot, aiming at meat-eating cockroaches that scuttle over unidentified particles on our red tile floor. A solitary, insolent cockroach clings to the bathroom door, one tenacious limb gripping a groove in the woodwork. With his toe, Adam takes a violent stab at the ball, which flies at the door, squashing the cockroach, leaving it dangling. The ball bounces away, but Adam remains where he is. Apparently he's waiting for me to fetch it. Which I do, returning the ball with an insouciance that hopefully preserves some of my dignity. In our two months together, although I haven't witnessed hostility, Adam has carried himself with a belligerent ferocity that reminds me of the glass-breaking thug in the movie *Trainspotting*.

Mr. Hou calls our names from the other side of the screen door. "You guys have a new housemate," he says with a lisp. His hair has been dyed black, which looks strange considering that he's over seventy and his face is wrinkled. He was probably attractive in his younger years. "No more funny business. No more drugs."

"Nobody was using drugs. Iggie and Steve just *seemed* like they were on something," says Adam.

"I like you Adam, but this is your last chance. No more hiring. No more training. If this doesn't work, I'm selling the franchise and I'm firing everyone. I'm going to start a kindergarten," Mr. Hou says.

"You're just busting my nuts," Adam says. "You won't fire us."

"I'm not busting your balls. I've had enough. You'd better make him feel welcome. He's getting his bags from the taxi. He's North American, too. He's a nice guy like you, John," he says, pointing in my direction. "No more teachers from England."

"I'm English," says Adam.

"You English are all drunks, drug abusers and sodomizers. I'm tired of you," Mr. Hou says. "Now behave. Samuel's here."

The new guy has a blond beard, is pear-shaped like me, but much taller and about thirty pounds heavier. He's standing on the other side of the screen door, his suitcases at his side, an expression on his face both dopey and abstractly intelligent. He's most likely heard everything. I don't know what he makes of it.

Adam and I are friends. Sort of. He's introduced me to his mates, all from some small district outside London. They're usually wasted on either ecstasy or booze. Except Adam. He's stayed away from the heavy drugs so far. He's also a very dedicated teacher, so for this reason Hou has kept him on for five years — the last two as Academic Director. He plays SimCity 4 on the computer and tells me about all the Chinese women he's shagged. I listen to him attentively. I prepare my English lessons. This is what I do. It's simple and it's enough. I'm happy.

But I can remember a time when I wasn't — happy, that is. In Toronto I was a mope. It doesn't matter why. When you're happy, especially after a long period of misery, you have two thoughts: why so miserable in the past? You also doubt whether things could get much better and sense that, in fact, they can only get worse.

Why am I here? I stumbled upon this advertisement in the Toronto daily Metro:

Teachers in Taipei, Taiwan needed!

Do you want to meet friends? Visit a foreign country? Be part of an exciting organization that pays well and that will provide on the job training? Call (416) 975 0092.

I believe in entropy. There's a set amount of energy in any contained area. By this I'm referring to Taipei or maybe even our school. Perhaps even this apartment. The addition of a new variable can cause the entire system to become a discordant flux. The new guy's threatening to upset the dynamic. You see, this is at the heart of my current anxieties. I'm aware of how things are with three people. Usually one person is the object of ridicule, even if it's subtle. With three people, someone is always pushed to the margins. I'll end up working hard to counterbalance Adam's Machiavellian tendencies. Samuel will quit or have a mental breakdown and then what are we going to do?

"If you have any problems, Samuel. Like if this guy here is keeping you up at night." Hou is pointing at Adam. "You'll let me know, okay? Call me anytime. I'll let you gentlemen acquaint yourselves." He says this last part with one foot out the door.

"Hi, I'm John," I say.

"Hi. I'm Samuel." The new guy wraps his massive purple hand around mine, rigorously pumps, and then does the same to Adam. He gives us a toothy smile.

"I'm Adam. Do you mind if I don't call you Samuel?" Adam says. "I think I'll call you America, instead."

Samuel is wearing flip-flops and he's carrying a bag of noodles in a Styrofoam bowl. "I guess I don't care. I'm a little hungry," he says sitting down to eat. "There wasn't enough on the plane."

"Go right ahead and eat, America," says Adam.

Samuel pulls chopsticks from his backpack. He pinches the noodles with resolve but they slither off the wooden chopsticks and land on his lap. Eventually he lifts the bowl oafishly with his hands and swallows a mouthful. After he's finished he stuffs the chopsticks into his pants.

"Aren't you going to wipe off the juice?" I say.

Samuel smiles. "Why are there clothes all over the place?" He's pointing to Adam's briefs, which are hanging on the computer monitor.

"They're Adam's."

"But why?" says Samuel.

"Because it's humid. It often rains in Taipei," says Adam.

I shrug. Adam believes that mildew grows on his T-shirts and socks and his clothes rot in his drawer, so he hangs them all over our apartment. I open the fridge and I'm confronted with his underwear. I have to move his sweater to watch TV. I brush aside his socks whenever I'm getting a glass from the cupboard. This is annoying but I don't complain. Adam doesn't respond well to constructive criticism.

Samuel sits down at a table, takes a calligraphy set from his backpack and practices writing Chinese characters. "I'd like to get a lot of studying done while I'm here," he says. "I studied Mandarin while I was at the University of Colorado."

"This is brilliant," Adam says. He's picking at his toenails with his fingers. He works at a sizeable clipping and eventually tears it off, then gets to his feet. "You see, we're surrounded by Chinese culture but in our very midst we get a little of America." With incisors bared, he hunches over Samuel. His gold chain hangs in Samuel's face. "Are you writing actual characters? You don't act like people in Hollywood, do you America? You think you're actually Taiwanese."

After an hour Samuel drops his pen and puts away the calligraphy paper. He mumbles something about third down and five, and then scans the sports section of a *USA Today*. He's aware that I'm watching him, so he puts the paper in his backpack.

"Are you coming to the pub?" Adam says. "It's your first night in town. Let's get you initiated."

"I'm suffering from jet lag," Samuel says. "I won't be much fun."

"Don't worry. I'll be enough fun for the three of us," Adam says.

What I love about being in Taipei is that I'm a part of *something* — how after evening classes we sit in the park on the benches next to the palm trees, with a bag of Taiwan beer, sometimes smoking weed even though signs at the airport read: *Anyone caught with illegal drugs will be executed*. Still full of beans because we've just finished class, the last fifteen minutes on the topic of differences, always differences, those between us and them; *dojiang* versus milk; the number four versus thirteen; senior homes versus children taking care of their elderly parents; how second-hand furniture is sometimes tasteful in the U.K., but here it is taboo; fat North American rumps versus their flat Asian counterparts (my students laughing then, pointing at mine as evidence). Our company, Hou's English School, is comprised of three Taiwanese secretaries, three foreign-born male teachers, and one frumpy woman from Manchester, who lives in Hou's other apartment with Hou's niece. She's lots of fun because we have no desire to sleep with her. Expats who teach at the local schools in Taipei are young men in their twenties from the U.S., Canada or the U.K., sometimes South Africa or New Zealand — a few like Adam having stayed too long and gone batty as a result. After class we climb on scooters and go to the Titanic Pub, if lucky with a secretary in tow, practically piggybacking, as we weave around cars at the traffic lights, riding in formation.

Samuel's obviously tired but he's making the trip with us. He's riding with Adam, on the back of his motorcycle. At the Titanic Pub we greet the other teachers. But we present a united front. This gives me pride, not the nationalistic variety, but one that has developed out of an awareness that we work at Hou's English School, the highest paying, most prestigious *bushiban* on the island. Knowing that I make twice as much as some of the other misguided ex-pats, I walk into the pub with a swagger. Our contract is that much better because, unlike other foreign teachers, we don't have to pay rent. I love teaching. I put ample time into my lesson plans. Teachers wear ties at Hou's English School — well, all but Adam, who says he's never given a fuck about proper work attire. You'd have thought others would have followed his lead — he is after all our Academic Director. At Hou's English School we also have to have graduated from university. Adam, of course, hasn't, but he's done a brilliant job of forging a degree from Cambridge — has, as a matter of limited public knowledge, paid for the transcripts off the Internet.

Samuel, now snug on a bench between two Englishmen, one of them Adam, is waiting his turn at darts, looking as if he'd rather be practicing his characters.

"He was answering me just using *phrases*," says Adam. "I asked him to answer in complete sentences. I said, 'When did you eat dinner today, Guo?' He said, 'After I came home from school.' I told the little tosser to give me the entire thing, not just the first phrase."

"Actually," Samuel interrupts, "it's a fragment."

"What'd you say, America?"

"It's a fragment. Actually a subordinate clause to be exact. An adverb clause. Time clause to be even more precise." Samuel's glasses are wiggling now. "Phrases lack a subject or a verb. 'After I came home from school,' has both."

"Are you being wise?"

"Excuse me?"

"Are you trying to teach *me* English? Five hundred years ago, Shakespeare was doing his thing. You were speaking Apache or some kind of foolishness. Who the fuck are you to teach me the Queen's tongue?"

I take the dart from Adam. He'd been twirling it in his hand, and was poised to jam it in Samuel's ear. "Look Samuel," I say. "It's a phrase. You're wrong. Cut it out, man."

Clearly, Samuel, his elephant-sized eyes watery, hasn't seen Ben Kingsley in *Sexy Beast* because he says, "Check the *Betty Azar*, the blue textbook, one of the later chapters, I think." At least he isn't making eye contact — never make eye contact, and turn your back first chance are techniques of self-preservation that have gotten me this far.

"Yeah, I'll *check* the fucking *Betty Azar*," says Adam. This is lame, especially since Samuel, who is paying his tab at the bar, hasn't heard him.

Adam and I stumble home at two o'clock. Adam, hand on crotch, runs to the balcony to relieve himself. Samuel has placed a Buddhist shrine on the mantel piece under Adam's Union Jack. Incense burns directly under it. I rush over and snuff it out with my sleeve. I upend the shrine, cradle it in my biceps, and take it to Samuel's room, where he's studying Chinese characters. "This isn't the best thing to be near Adam's flag," I say.

"You don't have to take it down," he says.

"Yeah, I probably should."

I go out to check on Adam. He's singing the Star Spangled Banner and peeing over the balcony. This is making a lot of noise because the awning below is tinny. I sing with him and try to match his volume but my voice lacks conviction. The concrete buildings in direct view are all drably built. They're also coloured a soot-black because the wind blows pollution onto them. Even still, they fascinate me. Who is on the other side?

Samuel joins us on the balcony.

"Just takin' the piss, America. Hope you take no offense." A cat is creeping onto the flat part of our roof. "Look America, I'm willing to concede that your culture — that is, Hollywood — has influenced the world more than anything coming out of the UK. Isn't there anything you want to tell us about your mates or way of life back home? You're such a mystery, America. What's the U.S. of A. all about anyway? Why don't you give us a feel for America?"

"I need to get some sleep," Samuel says. He goes back to his room.

"How about a feel for America," Adam slurs.

Five minutes before class, I'm writing on my white board. A desk at the other end of the room is askew so I straighten it. From back here I see that the students won't be able to read the past participles, written in faint green, on the white board. I erase them, careful not to take out any of the other colours. I'm printing them in blue now. Frantically, because I don't have a lot of time, but it also needs to be neat. If not, I'll have to start over again. Some of my intermediate students are streaming into the room. I'm looking over my shoulder. "Winny," I say. "You're with Ricky." They're both single parents in their forties. Why not match-make? "Jupiter, you're with Wynona." I've noticed Jupiter has been sitting with Greta, who's younger too and they've been speaking too much Chinese lately. Wynona's in her 60s and loves to learn. 7:00 now. I can't wait for anyone else. If they're late, though, that's okay. "How are you? Nice day? Let's start with the warmer. Ask the questions. English, Jupiter, English. Full sentences, Joanna. We're doing the present perfect. Ask the first in the present perfect and the second question in past tense. Use the past participles. The constructions are on the board. It's going to be a great evening. I'm really excited," I say. I say this every night. The Chinese have a smell, probably sweat — tofu and chilies secreted through their skin — that I can't get enough of. I'd like to bottle it and sprinkle it throughout our apartment. When my tiny classroom fills up with enough people, the scent's there within a few minutes. When everyone files out at the end of class I sit in my chair and inhale.

There's some yelling in the hallway that I'm ignoring now because everything's going well and because I get to teach the present perfect tonight — a grammar lesson with some interesting role-plays. The office role-play. The son/ daughter coming home late at night role-play. Plus, my tape-recorder's all set. They will listen to the South African accent tonight. I have memorized a new line in Chinese and I'm going to pounce on the first opportunity in class to use it. Surprise them a little. Someone's yelling in the hallway. It's just barely audible above the din of my class — my student's voices are reaching a crescendo now. "Have you been to Yang Ming Shan?" "Yes I have." "When did you go?" "I went in June." I always wait for the energy in the classroom to peak before I move on. This keeps the pace moving. More noise outside. I open my door and stick my head in the hall.

Adam is there. His knee is propping Samuel's door open.

"Why are you yelling?" I ask.

"His board isn't ready. Plus, he's insisting on groups of six. This is fucking unacceptable. Pairs or groups of three. He's got to comply or this is going to be a serious fucking issue." Adam looks warily in my direction. "Oi. There's ash from incense all over the Union Jack. Did you know about this?"

"No."

Adam has turned toward Samuel, who is out of my line of sight. I can feel his large presence on the other side of the door. "I'd like to see you after class," he says. Less loudly now.

I return to my room. Mr. Hou is by the potted fern in the corner, looking through the green leaves, which is creepy. He's silently judging what has just transpired.

"Have you ever taught kindergarten?" He says this to me conspiratorially.

Adam and I are on our balcony. He's Hawkeye Pierce to my Honeycutt. Our gaudy Hawaiian shirts are a testament to this. His idea, not mine. "What do you think of America?" Adam says.

"He's a nice guy."

"I think he's a fucking tosser."

"Oh God," I say. "Could you give him a chance?"

"Are you siding with your fellow American?"

"I don't care about any of that, Adam. I think he's a nice guy. Give him a chance. He's a little different. There's no crime in that."

Samuel's in front of a vegetable market on the ground floor of our building. Adam and I are looking down at him from our second floor balcony. Adam says that he could easily spit on the broccoli — the shop owner would think it was drizzle from the three-day shower that just ended. The owner is hosing down the area in front of his shop. A stream of slop, the colour of miso soup, is flowing under the rickety chair that Samuel's sitting on, sloshing against the sides of his Converse shoes. He gets up because a stocky man in a soiled white T-shirt is carrying a crate full of pears under the awning. The corner of the crate nicks Samuel's large head. He rubs his scalp and checks to see if there's blood on his hand.

"America is mixing with the Taiwanese," Adam says. "Just listen."

Samuel is slumping in his seat, loosely holding a Mah Jong set at his side. "*Wo ke yi gen ni men lian xi?*" Each syllable leaks out of his mouth. His eyes are pleading.

"I'm sorry. I have no idea what you're saying. Do you know how to play?" says an old man, a fisherman's cap screwed tightly to his head.

"*Wo yao gen ni men lian xi wo de Zhong wen,*" Samuel says, speaking in a deliberate manner — trying to nail each of the four tones, and when he can't, he starts the sentence all over again, which makes Adam snicker.

"It's okay. I speak perfect English," says the old man.

Samuel grabs a leg of the man's chair and spins it so they're facing each other. He's that oversized kid in school who doesn't realize how strong he is. "*Wo yao lian xi wo de Zhong wen.*"

"That big fuckwit doesn't know the first thing about Mandarin," says Adam, whose own Chinese, he always boasts, was learned the proper way — by shagging as many Taiwanese women as possible.

The elderly Chinese man is saying something to his friends. Samuel adjusts his voice a few decibels louder and repeats himself. They are speaking at the same time, Samuel's face reddening to a shade of mango. He inches his chair closer and moves his arms in supplication. The elderly man is bobbing up and down, as if he's barking orders.

"Let it go," calls Adam. He's on his tiptoes and all of his weight is leaning against the flimsy rail. If I stand next to him we'll surely plummet onto the mah-jong board.

"Let the man save face, America," he says.

Samuel glances up. But Adam isn't at the forefront of his consciousness. He's waving his arms at the elderly man, who by now has completely shut down. He's crossed his arms and is repeating, "I can't understand you."

"Drop it, America," Adam calls. "Let the man be."

Samuel looks up at us again.

"Maybe you should just let him sort this out," I say. I pull Adam away from the rail.

"What the fuck? Why? He's tormenting the old guy." He looks at me strangely.

The phone is mercifully ringing.

"Go get the fucking phone, John," he says.

I let go of Adam's arm. "Just leave him alone," I say rather pathetically. I get up from the rusty beach chair and get the phone.

"Can I speak to Samuel?"

"Actually, he's not here. He'll be in soon. Can I take a message?"

"It's Samuel's father. Can you write this down? He'll understand. Tell him we're going to stick it to them on Sunday. Nobody can stop our blitz. Our boy's going to pick apart their defense."

I write this down on a piece of paper. Adam's looking over my shoulder. "What's that about?"

"I have no idea. Samuel's father wants Samuel to call him before some game on Sunday."

Samuel's in the apartment now, sweating profusely. He takes off his shoes and from two yards away I can smell his socks.

"Your father gave John a bizarre message," Adam says.

I give it to Samuel. "Your dad laughed like it was the funniest thing in the world, though I don't see what's so funny. Did I mess up the message?"

"No, you did just fine," Samuel says.

Adam has been asking me for a long time to play indoor soccer with him. I always tell him that I'm not fond of the game. Truth is, there's a glint in Adam's eye, full of malice, which has made me reluctant.

After receiving the cryptic message from his father, Samuel can't concentrate on writing characters, so they arrange the sofa in a way that it serves as a goal and Adam kicks balls at him. Although Adam is tiny, he strikes the ball hard. Some of the shots bounce off Samuel's shoulder and stomach. The large man adroitly punches some of the shots back to Adam.

"You want to see what England is all about? We're about football. Not the American kind though."

Adam drills a shot at his head. Samuel catches it and stands there, placid, refusing to return the ball. At any moment Adam's likely to end the standoff. To hammer the ball from Samuel's clutch with his fist — perhaps a brief struggle, blood gushing from Samuel's nose, me mopping it up, stroking his head, telling him that this is just Adam's way.

I act quickly — put on my scooter helmet, and am in front of Samuel, asking him to relinquish the ball so that I can relieve him in net. Thank the Lord Buddha he hands it over. I'll explain to my students that the bruises on my forearms are from a spill on my scooter.

Samuel comes home the next morning after class with a forlorn look and a bag full of blue cans of Taiwan beer. "Guess where I was last night?"

His routine is to pull out his calligraphy set and study quietly in the corner of the room, his heavy breathing alone to remind us of his presence. Today, though, he slumps on the sofa. He's waiting for one of us to say something.

"I've no idea," I say.

"Not a clue, America," says Adam.

"I had a really bad night. I thought Fei and I were going to a karaoke."

"Where did you go?" says Adam.

"There were all these women. But there weren't any screens for the words, so I don't know. They didn't touch me or anything but they didn't look right. They had on lots of perfume. I was choking. I know it wasn't karaoke because there was dirt everywhere. Most KTVs are clean, right?"

"I've been in some dodgy KTVs," says Adam.

"Fei was chewing betel nut. He straddled this one girl and they didn't ask me at first for money for the beer I drank, which made me wonder. I gave them some money, and this one girl told me it wasn't enough so I gave her some more and then I gave this other girl a lot of money and then I got out of there."

"I'm surprised, America," Adam says. "I thought you'd want to experience everything Chinese."

Samuel sighs. "This would never happen in Colorado."

He comes out of his room later. He's stuffed his shirt with small pillows around the shoulders, the one on his right side larger and lumpier than the other. He walks around the rest of the day that way.

"What's with the pillows, buddy?" I say.

"I'm getting ready for tonight. What are you doing around two o'clock tonight?"

"Sleeping. What's tonight?"

"Nothing." He shuffles to his room.

"Hey Samuel. Can I talk with you for a second?"

He looks at me with his big, sleepy eyes. "What's up, John?"

"It's just," I say, "that this can be such a nice place if there's some equilibrium. Do you know what I mean? Maybe if you just tried to piss him off less, we could make this work. The apartment. The school. Do you agree?"

"Let me think about it," Samuel says. He walks into his room. The walls are so thin that I can hear the thud of his body landing on his mattress.

It's three o'clock. I'm awake because Samuel is talking loudly in the living room. I come out in my underwear. He's sitting on the sofa watching television. Blue Taiwan beer cans surround his chair.

"Why are you so agitated?"

"Tonight I celebrate. This is the most important day of the year. There's John Elway." He points to the television, then leans over and throws up on the floor. "I'm gonna clean that up later." He burps. "I'm from Colorado. We've got some of the best linebackers in the country. That's why I never made first team."

"Look, maybe you should keep it down. You don't want to wake up Adam."

Samuel stands, swaying, and slaps me on the shoulder. "Don't worry about him. Why do you worry so much about him? Try to tackle me." In a stupor, he bumps into me and falls on a lamp.

Adam's in the room now. He looks jarringly harmless in his skin-tight T-shirt and briefs. "What the fuck?" he says.

"It's nothing, Adam. I'll take care of it. You go back to sleep." I'm pushing him toward his room.

He watches the TV for a few seconds and says, "Those blokes wear tight pants."

Adam and I are unsure what to do. Neither of us is drunk. We each have an early morning business class, but that isn't for a few hours. We take a beer from the plastic bag at Samuel's feet. "Now this is interesting," Adam says. "Looks like we got Celine Dion and Mick Jagger doing a duet together. I had no idea this was part of the show."

At 4 o'clock AM Samuel babbles, "Did you see that catch? That catch was amazing. I want to do it."

He picks up the soccer ball, pitches it to me and says, "Throw the ball to me. Throw it to me right here." His hands are in front of his chest, in catching position.

I throw it to him.

"See, this is how you catch a ball. With your fingers!" He wipes yellow vomit from his shirt. "Let's do the entire thing after huddle."

He turns around, bends at his waist and places the ball on the floor between his tree-trunk-sized legs. "Put your hands under my ass, Adam."

"Now hold on a second," Adam says.

Samuel holds the ball, which still rests on the floor, with two hands. His face pokes at us between his knees. With his face upside down, the muscles in his face droop. He affects a ninny British accent. "Come on, Adam. I'm going to go long. You want to see America. You want to get a feel for America. Now put your hands under my ass."

"I think I've seen enough." Adam gets up and walks past us. Samuel stands up and grabs Adam's wrist. He tugs lightly and Adam loses his balance, almost falling. "We're good, right, Adam?" he says.

"What do you mean?"

He's still holding on to Adam's wrist. "We're good . . . I hope. No more of this, right?"

Adam doesn't say anything. He retreats to his room and shuts the door.

Samuel takes down a pair of Adam's mildewy sweat pants from the curtain rod. He gets down on his knees and mops up the stringy vomit on the floor. I grab a Fred Perry shirt and help him wipe it up.

"These are fried noodles, right?"

"That's right."

I laugh and Samuel laughs, his large shoulders gently shaking. I get Adam's Union Jack, tear it from the wall — its fabric lighter than I'd imagined — and crouch down to put it on the quickly drying puddle of vomit. Samuel grabs my wrist. He has a powerful grip. "Why are you doing that? You're just going to make him angry," which is a valid point. He picks me up by the shoulders, "We've got a good thing here. You don't want to mess it up, do you? Put this in the washing machine." He points to Adam's vomit-soaked, moldy clothes. He resumes watching the game.

Lying in my bed, my mind is serene. I can't sleep though. Samuel's yelling obscenities. I guess the Broncos are losing.

THE MALADJUSTED

I CLIMB OUT OF MY FOURTH FLOOR window and onto the fire escape landing, where I look down the alley for Ming. Spring has come and it's starting to warm up a little. I'm wearing a white robe and flip-flops, and carrying a basket that is attached to a long rope. Inside the basket is the exact amount of money for a medium vegetarian pizza, a bottle of Pepsi and a side order of garlic bread. This is the special from Tony's. Like an old house-ridden Middle Eastern woman, I lower down the basket of money to Ming, who is standing below the fire escape. Ming is non-judgmental, waiting patiently on the ground, as if all his customers order in this way. He takes the money and places the food into the basket. I carefully pull my dinner towards the fourth floor, stopping just before it reaches the metal landing. I remove the box of pizza and bottle of Pepsi and the garlic bread and yank the basket over the rail. I lie down on the cool surface of the fire escape landing and rest my arm on the warm pizza box.

For the first fifteen days of each month I order a pizza from Tony's. Then I run out of money. Until the end of the month I live on crackers, canned tuna and tomatoes, which I buy in bulk. My belly fluctuates in size according to the time of month, just as a python's shape changes depending on what it has eaten.

I've got to find somewhere else to buy my groceries. Three weeks ago, as I was leaving Value Mart, I said goodbye to two men, probably fathers, who were waiting for a taxi. They gave me a look, from which I inferred that they thought this was strange. So I told them that I have a mental illness. They said that they were sorry. I refuse to go back there.

I don't watch TV. I have nothing in common with Chandler, Joey or Ross. My alley's good for entertainment. My fire escape is on the fourth floor and, because of some creepers — really weeds that I've tended that have climbed up from some dirt in three mouldy flowerpots — I am afforded some camouflage, allowing me to watch while being unobserved. The alley teems with life, with meth-heads providing the main drama. Look at them now. The one with the stringy blonde hair, all ninety pounds of him, has picked up a dead mouse and is holding it by its tail. The other has a garbage can lid, thrust out as a shield. He's trying to knock the rodent from the other kid's hand, his head craned back in revulsion.

Our building is like a horseshoe enclosing a patch of grass. My neighbours opposite, a man, a woman and their son, Joseph, are from the Philippines. Their apartment is immaculate, at least from what I can see. The mother doesn't go out much because, I think, she's afraid of the addicts. Then there's Ben, who lives kitty corner. He sleeps on a sofa in the superintendent's apartment. I'm trying to figure out whether or not he's aware of me. Sometimes he unnervingly stares in my direction (when I'm on the fire-escape) and it's a test of wills, more specifically a test as to whether I will stir, giving him proof of my existence. I always win. He eventually goes back inside. I don't like him very much. I guess if I were to think about it, and I have, it's that I don't think he'd like me. He ignores the family from the Philippines. He looks like the intolerant type, with his shaved head and long side burns, and tattoos on his neck.

How can I be sure he can't see me? One hot summer night last August, at three in the morning — I'm an insomniac by the way — I got up on the flat roof and crawled over to his corner of the alley. I looked across to my fire escape landing. I'd put my orange jacket, and jeans, both stuffed with pillows, in my camouflaged hideout. I was about two metres higher than his vantage point, but was confident that the line of vision was on par with that from his balcony. From there I couldn't make out any part of the orange jacket. It was night, I know, but he usually comes out at dusk. The moon was out, almost replicating the amount of light at seven o'clock PM

I despise Ben because he never says hi to Miriam or Joseph, the Filipino woman and her son, who live next to him. Granted, she never says anything to him, but it's his responsibility to be friendly, not hers. She doesn't speak English, but she seems nice enough. I've said hello to her twice, even making eye contact. Last March, when I said hello she didn't hear me. I tried again in May. She heard, or at least I think she did. She turned towards me and smiled, and then said something in her language. Tagalog?

Kim, my diligent, kind-hearted social worker, has been trying to get me to leave my apartment and engage with other people in this fine city. I've thwarted her by turning my apartment into a kind of carnival in an attempt to diminish any imperative on her part to get me to leave. Three and a half months ago I suspended toilet paper artfully from my ceiling to celebrate Christmas. I used six rolls. The strands of paper ran uniformly from the ceiling to an inch above the floor. I coloured the odd strand. She couldn't see the far end of the room where I was sitting, so she had to push through it to find me.

In late winter I chipped a hole in my living room wall and sat in my bedroom on the other side, hoping to surprise her when she arrived. In fact, I spent a whole hour feeling drained of energy and almost sedated. When she eventually let herself in (she has a key), I poked my shoulders through the brittle hole and wriggled out to the other side, dropping to her feet. "Ta da," I said, but she wasn't amused. I never got around to boarding up the wall, so it still has a hole.

This is my favourite time of the year. Every spring the Municipality of Toronto allows people to set out old and unwanted furniture, so under cover of the night I explore the neighbourhood stealthily, taking anything attractive that I can fit into my apartment. Just a while ago, I built a wall of furniture in my living area. The tangle of sofas, end tables and lamps proved a challenge for Kim, who is sixty-five years old, but after encouragement from me on the other side of the pile, she managed to climb on top of a sofa, which acted as the foundation. She looked disoriented at this point, so I took a lumpy mattress off the chairs and night tables, which let her through. I didn't want her taking too long and complaining too much.

Last week I made a maze with accumulated shelves, desks and kitchenware. I'm learning which pieces fit best with others to create passageways and dark entrances to confuse her. A large pool tarp and a few musty blankets give the whole thing a cover. When she arrived last Tuesday she dropped to her knees to contemplate the maze. She's quite fit for her age, but even so, she surged ahead clumsily. She made her way through with a smile on her face, but eventually called out for my help. She was breathing heavily, struggling through a tunnel between a coffee table and three end tables.

"Come on Kim," I said. "Just a little farther. Almost there."

At the end of my maze waited a cup of mud, as I call it. I'm an ardent coffee drinker. I use my own machine. Smiling, Kim declined, like she always does, telling me that it was too strong. I set up a chessboard and we played late into the night. I beat her for the first time. She asked me if I wanted to go down to the local chess club to play with other people. I told her I didn't. She's still pressuring me, despite the maze.

She's married and has four grown children. Her husband retired a long time ago. She remains on staff part-time at WOLT so she can spend time with me. Her client list has dwindled, and yet she always comes to my place on Tuesday afternoons.

The temperature's dropped. I go inside and put on a hat and mittens and cover myself with a blanket. I'm reading the note my psychiatrist transcribed last Wednesday. He wants me to examine it for any distortions of thought.

In the grocery store everybody immediately is looking at me. They think my fedora looks ridiculous. It takes me two hours to buy only a few groceries. I keep on walking down the aisles looking for canned tomatoes but I can't find them. I'm a little dizzy and I must look funny. I take off my fancy hat but my scalp feels naked and my hair is really greasy, so I put it back on, but then I look ridiculous again. Two older ladies talk about me in the aisle but stop as soon as I walk close to them. One says something like, "He doesn't do anything on the weekend." I give the cashier four twenty-dollar bills to buy thirty-nine dollars worth of groceries. She gives me back two of the twenties and is laughing at me. I tell her I have a mental illness. She says that she is sorry. When I'm leaving she says, "Take care." Now everybody knows that I'm a nut.

My psychiatrist and Kim have been talking about me, but as Kim has pointed out, this isn't illegal or unethical because they inform me of everything they discuss. They've put together a "Get-Mike-out-into-the-world plan." It's all very wordy and convoluted, but from what I understand it should unfold like this. First step: Kim and I go to the local chess club by bus, look at the entrance, and then return. Second step: I enter the chess club and check out the interior to get a feel for the place. Third step: Kim and I go with our own chessboard and sit down to play together and then depart. Fourth step: I play a game of chess with another player.

We've torturously accomplished the first three. Tomorrow I'm going to strike up a mind-numbing game with someone other than Kim. I need to get some shuteye. If I eat too much pizza I won't sleep at all, but even knowing this I eat three more slices without chewing much. My stomach gives in to the dough, bloating more than usual. I don't have to check my movement now because Ben's nowhere to be seen and his lights are off anyway. I can't sleep due to an inability to surrender to oblivion, so I drag a sleeping bag out here on the fire escape to get some rest. A streetcar rumbles off in the distance. I don't believe in Heaven, or Last Judgment or even an afterlife. I believe this is all we have. So if you think about it, and I have, that makes every second of existence vital, so we can either lead an idle, hedonistic life, or we can help others, or we can do something interesting. I've wasted a lot of time, and knowing this makes me even more incapable of helping people or doing interesting things, which makes me more anxious. It's an irony that provokes a gentle laugh from both my psychiatrist and Kim; but their reaction makes me curl in anguish — I mean literally to curl over on my side. I feel a tingling surging from my neck, to my shoulders, and to my hands. I feel lonely, like I'm going to die alone. Everyone knows that anxiety causes cancer, but I think for about the five millionth time that at least I'm not Ben, and I have Kim for a friend.

It's now six o'clock. There are only seven more hours until step four. Six o'clock AM is a nice time of the day for me. I have some serene thoughts. Take, for example, my impact on the environment. I read in the Globe and Mail a study about the sustainability of the earth. According to U.N. calculations, in order for the earth to sustain itself, each person can only inflict 300 units of damage to the earth in a year (many factors go into this). People in Bangladesh do the least harm, with each Bangladeshi averaging about 200 units. North Americans on the other hand average one thousand units. My sustainability quotient is probably even less than 200. I live in a small, cramped apartment. I have saved space in landfill sites by hoarding used furniture. The amount of toxic waste that I have released into the atmosphere is negligible. I emit some flatulence that pollutes the ozone, but I travel on buses and refuse to get into Kim's car. I've tried drinking rain to save water. I only flush my toilet on Wednesday, Friday and Monday nights (before Kim comes on Tuesday). Pizza is my only indulgence, and since the ovens are fuelled by natural gas, even this isn't so bad. They're vegetarian and so no animals have died unnecessarily. It has crossed my mind to cut out cheese but it tastes too good. I read day-old newspapers, taken from the superintendent's blue bin. (He's also a jerk, but that's a whole other story.) I haven't hurt anyone's feelings in three years. I'm exceedingly polite and honest. So, in other words, if the world were populated by six billion Mikes (me) — a

Kantian thought experiment, a derivative of the categorical imperative that might be useful for anyone to try — there wouldn't be any global warming, or war, or traffic accidents. Everyone would say hello to everyone else. There'd just be an abundance of needless worry and smothering anxiety.

At last I'm stirring in my damp sleeping bag, and then glancing at my watch. It's one o'clock in the afternoon. Kim's going to be here any second so I need to have a shower and eat some more pizza, which I do.

Someone's knocking. I choose not to answer.

Then, Kim is standing in my doorway, sighing and looking at her watch. "Sorry," I say. "I was reluctant to get the door."

"How are you feeling, Mike?" she says.

"I didn't sleep well," I say. I have resisted calling her "Mom", an urge that I've had ever since I first called her that. She's never told me not to call her "Mom", although she did remind me once that I already had a mother and that she lives in North York. I know what she's going to say next.

"Then you'll sleep well tonight," she says. "We should get there early so that we can find someone to play."

This is the one difference between her and me. She worries about small earthly matters, my finances, being on time, getting me to put on a clean shirt, whereas I have more existential concerns. I can't imagine having her concerns, but, on the other hand, I can't imagine that she fully understands what goes on in my brain.

The bus is crowded and darn hot. I'm sticky and am dangerously close to a full-blown panic attack. At our stop we get out quickly, and I tell her that my new-found briskness of step has nothing to do with any desire to get in the Chess Hut, but with the extreme heat.

With understandable trepidation Kim and I enter the club, me carrying my own board. We stand on the fringe of the playing area, looking awkwardly for an opening. I want to sit down and play a game with Kim, but she refuses. I stare at each person — at the Korean man with the spiky hair, at the overweight lady with the glasses and chin hair and at the man with the grey sweat pants. I should be staring at the boards, curious as to how each game is unfolding, but instead I stare into people's faces. This makes them uncomfortable but I can't stop myself. There is some quiet chatter, spoken in a language only understood by people who understand chess.

"Who wants to play?" I say. Everyone looks at me.

Just as we are about to give up and set up our own board, a man, about thirty-five years old, crosses the room and asks if I want to play. This man is clearly an angel (if angels exist). I inform him that we're probably mismatched, and then realize that he might take this as a sign of arrogance, so I say, "What I mean is that I'm the weaker player, not you." He shushes me and guides me to a table and shows me my side of the board. Kim stays in the room but watches from a distance. She feigns interest in a couple of games while keeping an eye on me.

I tell him I have a mental illness.

"Do you hear voices?"

"No, but sometimes I feel a bit maladjusted."

"Do you hallucinate?"

"I don't think so. I once was convinced that the ozone layer was going to rupture and that everybody would die. I've since read that the ozone layer is starting to heal itself. So I feel better."

"I hear voices," he says, matter-of-factly. "If I can concentrate on my moves I can drown them out. Do you know what I'm talking about?"

"I think so."

"Let's play chess."

"All right."

I play my first couple of moves quickly. I play white and lead with my king's pawn. I set up a Guico Piano. I also castle on my king's side. My opponent castles queen's side and pushes up two pawns in attack. His knight supports one of the pawns. His rook runs a line straight through to my king. This prevents me from taking one of the pawns. I remain quiet. I slow down on my moves and I stop rubbing the bit of stubble under my nose. I also stop looking over to Kim. Eventually, my opponent checkmates me with a formidable combination queen, pawn and knight. He tells me I've extended myself too much. "Never attack into my area until you have the middle of the board secured, with your pieces supporting each other." I listen intently, only interrupting the man once, before running over to Kim. I ask her for a piece of paper and a pen. With a sheet torn out of her daily schedule and a pen, I return and say, "I want to get this down. This stuff is really good. Would you mind saying it again?"

I've been distracted for thirty minutes, without metacognitive awareness. It's a pleasant respite, really. Kim and I leave together. On the way out I pass a couple of people, who are in the middle of a long and drawn-out battle, and say, "I'll see you guys next time." They are concentrating heavily on their game. I don't think they hear me.

When we get on the bus, I turn to Kim. "I'd like to go back there again tonight, if it's okay with you."

"I'm busy tonight but we can do it another day."

"Maybe I'll go back there by myself."

I might not go, I know, but I want to go home and think about it. I want to put together a plan.

THAT'S VERY OBSERVANT OF YOU

ON A COOL SPRING DAY, MELANIE TRUDGED into the Lucky Dragon Restaurant with a videocassette tucked under her arm. She ordered two portions of dumplings and pork fried rice and sat down at a small table. The place was empty until a group of people came in and sat at one of the big round tables. A waiter, newly hired, appeared with her dinner on a plate. Melanie sprung from her seat, and said, "No, I'm not eating here. I always get takeout." She smiled nervously and said, "My friend is waiting for me outside. I'm sorry. This is my fault, but I need it wrapped for take-out."

The waiter obediently put the rice and dumplings in a Styrofoam container. As he was handing it over, Melanie, her hand instinctively flattening a stray mousy clump of hair sprung awry, and then shielding three tiny craters to the right of her thin lips, said, "My friend really likes extra peanut sauce if you don't mind."

Outside, she stood on the sidewalk and peered through the window, staring at the waiter. Loose change in his pockets pulled his belt down so she could see the shape of his hipbone through his jockey shorts. His dark-brown, neatly trimmed beard complimented his handsome, Slavic-looking face. He deftly balanced a tray of squid and broccoli with one hand and with the other carried a pitcher of water. Melanie thought that it was the nicest thing for them to have hired a Caucasian man. She didn't speak Mandarin after all, and although when ordering she could indicate her dish of choice by writing down the corresponding item number on a pad, she felt more comfortable now that she could communicate verbally with someone, with this nice man. *What can I say to him?*

After getting off the streetcar near her apartment, she dropped the video clumsily beneath the exhaust pipe of a red '98 Pontiac. This was *her* designated spot. *Oh dear, I've got to speak to them about this. They can't park here. It's completely unacceptable!*

Melanie ran into her neighbour and her ponytailed boyfriend in the hallway. The boyfriend fumbled with his keys at the door, *most likely the keys to his red Pontiac,* and hauled a bag of groceries into apartment B. Her neighbour, a friendly lady, about thirty, asked Melanie what movie she was going to watch.

"Romancing the Stone," Melanie said, staring at the boyfriend.

"We're having friends over," the woman said. "After you're finished eating and watching your movie, would you like to come over for a drink?"

"I can't. I'm not even watching this. I'm going out with my sister. I've just got to drop this off and then I'm leaving. We're going dancing." She smiled, rushed into her apartment and shut the door.

Melanie killed all the lights, removed her spring jacket and tiptoed around her apartment. She lowered the volume of the movie, so that it was barely audible, and sat on her knees a few inches in front of the television. One of her hands moved mechanically from the potato-chip bag to her mouth. Her fingers rubbed grease into the folds of her flabby belly and legs. She imagined she was in her parents' home in Maplehorn, thinking up another hiding position, her chin on the ground adjacent to the baseboard and the accumulated grime, suppressing a sneeze so as not to give her sister a clue as to where she was, then moving to the next hideout, her sister unfairly discontinuing the count at seventeen when she was supposed to count to twenty-five. Now she was crying inconsolably. Thoughts of her sister — the only person in the world who loved her — made her cry, but then she stopped, thinking that the lovely, bearded, Slavic-looking waiter probably didn't like women who excessively cried. But then, on second thought, it was nice to think about her sister, so she continued to quietly sob — God it felt good! — and waiter be screwed if he didn't like sensitive women. Ponytailed man also be screwed. How dare he park in her spot! He probably assumed she wouldn't mind. Well, of course she cared. She can't get carried away, though. Her neighbours might hear her, and, oh God, that would be awful! She carried a flashlight so she could find her barrette and so she could read her R.T. Williams mystery book. She lay on her carpet, reading and intermittently using the binding of her book to scratch the large folds of her mid-section.

Towards midnight, just as the party next door was winding down, Melanie sat in her shower with the hot water streaming on her head. She held her R.T. Williams mystery novel away from the water and read until the hot water ran out. She lay in a way she believed made her more attractive — her bottom on the bathroom floor, flattened and no longer sagging, her belly, concave at the rib cage, her hair and face wet. She wished that the lovely waiter could see her like this. She was optimistic for a moment that one day he *would* see her in this sensual position. Why not? Becky Charles had a husband. What could she say to him? It had to be a casual remark, yet intimate enough for him to notice her.

Before sleep, Melanie was tucked under her covers with the phone cradled against her neck. "He's the nicest man. You should see him, Nicole . . . " "Oh, I could never do that . . . " "What? All alone? No, I never eat alone . . . " "No, it's simply a bad idea. You've got to come here so that we can go there *together.*"

Melanie spread out her lunch on the floor as if she were on a picnic: a tub of cottage cheese, four slices of pizza, two cartons of milk and a muffin. Anyone passing by would not be able to see her through the tiny window at the top of the door. When Becky Charles walked into the boardroom with an urn of coffee on a cart, Melanie shuddered in fear, and backed herself into a corner. She felt like a trapped squirrel. Despite assurances from Becky to go on eating, she gathered the cottage cheese and pizza into her purse. Pieces of cheese and sauce spilled, and she had a fleeting, distorted thought — that Becky might confiscate her lunch. On the way out she mentioned that her friends from accounting usually ate with her, though she didn't know why she'd lied to Becky — Becky, the one nice salesperson in the company, Becky, the sweet middle-aged lady who always offered her a ride home, and who always wished her a nice weekend.

Melanie ran back into the room. In a hushed voice, she said, "Actually, I've been eating alone in this room every day, Becky. Can we keep this between the two of us?"

Melanie walked slowly behind her sister down the hallway of the apartment building, hoping that she might get to introduce Nicole to the neighbours, not to the man with the ponytail, but to his girlfriend, the woman who'd invited her to the party. *They probably don't think I even have a sister. Well, they can see with their own eyes not only that I have a sister, but that we have the same bouncy, red curls and unaffected smile and grace, a gift from daddy and that she's about the best sister anyone in this world could have and that the two of us together are a team.*

At the Lucky Dragon Restaurant Melanie and Nicole took a seat at one of the round tables and looked at the menus. Nicole said she needed to wash her hands, and then got up and went to the washroom. Unfortunately, the waiter chose this moment to take their order. Melanie sniffed sadly. "Would you mind coming back? My sister was just here. She's in the washroom."

When her sister returned, the nice-looking waiter asked them if they were ready to order. With her hand reflexively covering the pockmarks on her cheeks, Melanie introduced her sister to him and ordered a plate of *gong bao* chicken.

Melanie had difficulty responding to her sister's inquiries about her job during dinner because she was trying to think about what she might say to the waiter when he returned.

"Why don't you ever eat here alone, Mel?" said Nicole.

"Oh I could never do that! I mean — where would I sit?"

Nicole pointed to an older woman in a corner, eating by herself. Melanie first thought she was a businesswoman because she was wearing a suit, but on second thought she wasn't sure. The lady was reading a magazine, an *In Style* magazine that was suitable perhaps for someone creatively inclined. The lady was odd. She was alone, spread out as if she were sitting in her own sunroom. She had on a fuchsia blouse and suit jacket, her grey hair perfectly pinned, her eyelashes done but not gaudily and yet here she was blowing her nose in public, not discarding the tissue in her purse but placing the bacteria-infected rag next to her plate of fried noodles — and she was doing this entirely unselfconsciously. Melanie thought, I could *be* this woman. "Do you think she looks distinguished, Nicole? Do you think she's married?"

Nicole patiently answered these questions, and then said, "Why don't we invite her to sit with us, Melanie?"

"Oh God," Melanie said. "If you did that, I'd die of embarrassment."

Melanie was at her desk organizing a meeting with CIBC, but also listening to Becky Charles, whose large front teeth were shiny white. "I've been so tired," Becky said. "You know, the long hours here and then my children, bless them, are growing into their bodies, and their hormones are raging. I *really* needed some time to myself. You're going to think I'm totally spoiled, but I booked a weekend at the Beild House Country Inn and Spa in Collingwood. Joe took the children for the weekend so there was no one to burden me when I ate, and I could get tipsy on red wine. I met this woman, Linda, who's about my age and we had a wonderful time, taking long walks in the garden and sharing our life-stories."

"Really?" Melanie said.

"Like I said, I needed some time for myself. Some *me* time. I think sometimes that I'm my own best company. You know what I mean?"

The phone ringing in the next cubicle irked Melanie. *I do know what you mean, Becky. You're talking about human dignity, right? We all have dignity — you're a very strong woman, Becky Charles, and don't worry because I will never, ever steal your dignity. You'd have loved to meet this lady, oh, I never actually got her name, but she was at the Lucky Dragon Restaurant with my sister and me the other day and she reminded me exactly of you. She was a powerful person, too. I wish I'd gotten to know more about her. I wish that I could have told her what kind of impression she left on me. We all have our dignity. You were so nice to me when you caught me in the boardroom, eating where I wasn't allowed. You have a kind heart, Becky.*

Melanie rarely spoke to anyone at work, but today she got up from her chair, and walked over to Becky, who looked unnecessarily taken aback, her eyebrows raised, her supple lips formed into an 'O'. A palpable shock ran from woman to woman. Oh God, thought Melanie, this was embarrassing. She gathered a faint steam of courage, and said, "Could you get me a brochure for that hotel?"

It was Sunday night. With a touch of blush hiding the scars on her face, and adorned with a recently purchased brown leather coat, Melanie walked Spadina Avenue, first to Dundas Street and then back to College Street, her eyes fixed on the yellow neon sign, LUCKY DRAGON RESTAURANT, and below, the Chinese characters. She thought, *this is just like going to get my haircut — there's no reason for it to go badly. Nicole is praying for me. She wants this oh so bad to turn out okay for me so I have to do this for her, really. Oh, let's just get it over with. I just want to eat, right? I make money like any normal person, and I need to eat or I'll be hungry, right?*

The handsome waiter packed her dumplings and fried rice in a bag. When he handed it to her, Melanie said, "Actually, I'd prefer to eat here tonight if that's okay."

"Of course it's all right." The waiter smiled. His dark-brown beard glistened.

She motioned to grab the bag so she could take it to a table, but he told her that he'd do that for her, and that she could eat with a knife and fork or chopsticks if she so desired. At the table Melanie used her R.T. Williams mystery novel as a shield. When the waiter asked her what she wanted to drink, she didn't lower it. She asked for a glass of water, her words muffled by the paperback just inches from her face. When he brought her food, she said, "Thanks." The waiter smiled and this calmed her. *Oh, what did I want to say to him?*

Melanie slowly chewed her dumplings. From behind her novel she watched a couple eating in a corner of the restaurant. The man and the woman had at no point during their dinner spoken to each other except to ask about pedantic matters such as the amount of the bill and the way to the washroom. Again, she began to think about the woman with the *In Style* magazine and about Becky Charles. The imagined conversations, and the insightful remarks by her in her daydreams left her with a faint smile on her lips. Her mood improved considerably. She came to an understanding — what she thought of as an epiphany — that no one was watching her and that nobody noticed her. Sitting down in the restaurant had indeed been difficult, but once at her table, she realized that she didn't stand out. She was in a comfortable environment, where she could wipe chili sauce from the bottle so it wouldn't stain the marble table, where she could stab each piece of *shui jiao* and plunk it in her mouth, and swirl the chopsticks in the rice, these actions as natural as a female cat licking the dust and hairballs from her fur. And best of all was that the food tasted as good as take-out. Now, all she had to do was get the ball rolling — the waiter probably wanted to talk to her just as much as she wanted to talk with him.

She left the Lucky Dragon without saying anything to him but promised herself that next week she would.

The next day Melanie got up from her cubicle, and stood in front of Becky's desk. "I went to the Lucky Dragon Restaurant last night," she said. And then hastily added, "My friend came with me." She went back to her desk. Five minutes later Melanie returned to Becky's desk to tell her that what she'd said earlier hadn't been true and that she hadn't eaten with a friend, that she'd gone by herself. "I needed some time for myself. I'm feeling really good these days."

"That's great, Melanie."

Melanie thought that Becky's reaction this time had been considerate. In her look had been the right amount of interest, and no sign of wanting to cut off the conversation.

This was the second Sunday in a row that Melanie ate alone at the Lucky Dragon. The waiter with the dark-brown beard rhythmically tapped a pencil on a note-pad, and asked her what she wanted for dinner.

She knew her sister was praying for her. She ordered some fried noodles, and then with the precision that comes with rehearsal, she said, "Hi, I'm Melanie. I've wanted to introduce myself to you for a while."

"Hi, Melanie. It's nice to meet you."

"You look busy today," she said.

He looked around at the half-empty restaurant, raised his eyebrows in a bored manner, and then caustically said, "That's very observant of you."

Melanie missed her streetcar stop on the way home that night. She rode three extra stops and had to double back east to get to her apartment. In the building she got off at the wrong floor and decided to walk up the flight of stairs instead of waiting for another elevator. The superintendent hadn't fixed the malfunctioning light in the elevator, and of course someone had tracked dirt in here and so why wouldn't she be distracted? *Oh I wish I'd said something clever to that waiter!* Inside her apartment she couldn't remember eating her fried noodles and she agonized as to whether she'd paid her bill or not. She called the Lucky Dragon and spoke with the owner. "I'm sorry," she said. "I've had a long day at work. I was just at your restaurant and I'm not sure if I paid."

The owner rifled through the receipts and found that she had.

She said, "Good," and then hung up.

She set her clock so that she could get to work early the next morning. After the alarm sounded she remembered the events of the night before, stared at her walls for forty minutes, and ended up being late.

Later that day, she discovered that somebody had parked in her designated parking space. *What kind of person does that?* The offending person was, of course, her neighbour's boyfriend, the ponytailed jerk who was over almost every night. She could put a note on the windshield of his car. She'd get the wording just right, but then she dismissed this. After all, if she acted, it would be their prerogative to react and she didn't want to — what was the saying? — lob the proverbial ball onto their court and give them the advantage. She thought

THAT'S VERY OBSERVANT OF YOU

about perhaps waiting for them in the dark, *perhaps behind a pillar, so as to casually come across them and mention that she needed the spot. They'd say, "We need it." She'd say, "You're being really unreasonable." The man then, the one with the loping gait and the jet-black hair tied back in a ponytail, would say, "Fuck if we care!"*

It's been mine for three years. I'd pay less rent if I didn't have it. I put some cones there, but they move them. I set up twenty-five cones, covering every square millimetre of my space, space that I can do whatever I want with. They drive over the cones. I put them back. They drive over them again, and then they find a cone on top of their car like a dunce cap, saying, how dare you drive over me, this space belongs to Melanie! If I wanted I could let a homeless man camp there. I could decorate it with flowers and put a patio set on it so I can read and have some lemonade now that it's getting warmer. People will take my side. We'll vote at the next meeting, and everyone'll vote for them to leave.

Melanie hadn't called Nicole for a few days, so she wasn't surprised that her sister phoned her at work, and said, "I think you should talk about it with them first, Mel, but if it'll make you feel less anxious, then I guess maybe you could call a tow truck."

"They're in my spot and it's Wednesday. It's not even the weekend. I can't even do my grocery shopping."

"Why do you care so much? You don't *own* a car. You can leave and do your shopping. They're not keeping you there. Will you please try to do something to ease your anxiety, Mel?"

~ 49 ~

"You're right. I can't seem to get it out of my head. I don't know what I can do though."

"Talk to them."

❧

When Nicole arrived, Melanie was frustrated because her neighbour's boyfriend *hadn't* parked in her spot. *How could they have known Nicole was coming? Are they listening in on my calls? They deliberately didn't park there to embarrass me in front of my sister, the one person who trusts me. They're trying to take away the one person who fully believes in me, and all that I'm worth. Together we're formidable. Wait till they see the wrath of my big sis.*

After dinner, with a panic attack imminent, Melanie watched from her doorway as Nicole knocked on the neighbour's door. The young woman answered, her boyfriend standing behind her.

"Sorry to bother you," Nicole said. "I'm Melanie's sister — the girl that lives down the hall — I was wondering if you could do us a favour. Could you please ask your guests not to park in her spot? I sometimes come down for the weekend and I need to park there and even though Melanie doesn't have a car she likes to keep it free."

"We didn't realize it was a problem," the man with the ponytail said. "We'll tell our friends not to park there. I've parked there myself before, but I won't anymore. I'm sorry if it's inconvenienced you or Melanie in the past."

By the time Nicole had pushed her into her apartment and had shut the door, Melanie was crying inaudible grotesque sobs.

"You need to tell people how you feel, Mel. You need to tell them your feelings before you get so upset. You have to work on your communication skills, or you're going to go through a lot of unnecessary heartache."

Melanie noticed that the waiter had a vaguely bloated stomach, not the loose, flabby waistline you find on middle-aged men, but the distended type on malnourished children. When he came over, she said, "Hi, do you remember me from a while ago? I said, 'You look busy.' And you said, 'That's very observant of you.' Well I happen to think that, 'That's very observant of you' is a clever retort. And while it's quite clever, I also think it's an inconsiderate and ill-tempered thing to say.

"You're an intelligent, physically attractive person but you lack sensitivity. The appropriate response on your behalf would've been to smile, maybe say, 'Enjoy your tea,' and then move on.

"Do you have any idea how easy — how *unoriginal* — it is to come up with a sarcastic comment like that? Do you know how easy it is to ridicule someone who, like me, was trying to initiate a conversation? A stranger asks me for the time and I could say, 'Why are you asking me?' and this person would probably feel awful. You may be thinking that you had absolutely no responsibility to talk with me that day, and I'd agree with you whole heartedly — but I also add that like this liberty, the freedom to mistreat whomever you want, I'm afforded a similar liberty, to come in here and tell you how I feel.

"You might be thinking that you should just get away from me. To this I say 'walk away!' However, having said all of this, I also want to say that for the last few weeks I've been staring at your lovely, thin hips and at your cute, tight bottom. And yes, if you'd asked nicely, I would have gone out with you.

Instead, you said 'That's very observant of you', and I went home and stared at my walls and got into fights with my sister and showed up late for work. I was so furious at you."

Melanie stopped. She was pleased, believing it had gone as well or better than the early afternoon dry run. When the waiter didn't immediately respond, she said, "How do you feel about everything I've just said?"

"I didn't mean to upset you, Melanie," he said. "I'm sorry if I did."

"Really? Perhaps I'm overreacting."

"We *could* meet for a drink after work," he said, "if you want."

"Maybe." She considered this. "I don't know. Do you think we can be friends?"

"Of course, we already *are* friends, Melanie."

The waiter walked away. She thought, *maybe I was a little too hard on him. Should I apologize?*

IN THE LOW POST

I HAVE THE BALL IN THE LOW post, my back to the basket. Adrian, a lanky eighteen-year-old kid, six foot six — his calves a third of this length — is draped over me. I pump fake and Adrian bites, leaving his feet. I dig my shoulder into his stomach and hook the ball over him, but even so he smacks it out of bounds. He knows better than to say anything. I grab his T-shirt and pretend like I'm going to slap him. "Just joking. Nice block, bro'." All ten of us stand waiting for the game to continue, no one saying the obvious — that it is, of course, my job to retrieve the ball. I'm not going to make an issue of it. I might have as a teenager, but I'm twenty-five now. I follow the ball over a clump of grass to a chain link fence, where it rolls up against a leg. I jump back a step. The leg belongs to a kid, who is lying still. With the sun setting he's difficult to see. His skin is lighter than mine. He's dirty and he smells like vomit. His lack of expression and unwillingness to call out as the ball hit his leg is what trips me up the most.

"What are you doing hiding over here, little bro'?"

"I'm not hiding," he says. "I'm taking a rest." He brushes flies from his face.

"Why don't you come on over? This here's my court. You can watch me dominate."

"That guy stuffed you."

"Well, that's a matter of interpretation. Are you coming?"

A flicker of hope on his face, he says, "Can I play you one on one?" He gets to his feet in one seamless motion, not even using his hands.

"You don't want to play with me," I say. "But if you come to the court you can see better."

"I don't feel like it. I'm just gonna rest." He lazily turns so that his back is against the fence, and drops to the ground with a thud. He rolls in the dirt, lying on his side.

"Suit yourself." Fuck him, I think. Social work is for social workers. I'm here for the run. My blood needs to rush through my veins. I get enough talk at the office. "See ya later, little bro'. By the way, what's your name?"

"Karl." He says this so softly that I wonder if he's even said it at all.

The next evening Karl gets up from the dirt and walks to the lamppost. He hugs its base and shimmies himself up with leverage from his legs, stomach and arms, like a squirrel climbing the trunk of a tree. From where I'm standing, his eyes and nose are exposed yet blurred by the light. He perches up there for half an hour, restlessly shifting his position as if he's looking for something. After a while we forget he's there.

But now he yells, "Can you see me?"

"Yeah we see you," I say. "Hang onto something, Karl. I don't want to scrape your guts off my court."

Karl unscrews one of the light bulbs, stretching his shirt so that he doesn't have to touch it directly. He puts it on top of the lamppost and waits for us to react.

"Ignore the little fucker," I say. "He just wants our attention." My soldiers obey me. We play in diminished light. Karl loosens a second bulb and in doing so he's shaking the post. The bulb on top rolls over the side and falls to the tarmac. Shards of glass spray the legs of Tilley and Manny, who are drinking slushies on the sidelines. Tilley walks over to the lamppost and tilts back his head to stare at Karl. I'm concerned that he might shake the post, causing Karl to topple from his nest. I yell at Karl myself, tell him to get the hell down. Just then this woman shows up. She's maybe thirty years old, maybe forty. It's hard to tell. Her hair's thinning in places and she's got a scowl on her face.

"Get on down from there, Karl," she says. "What's he doing up there?" She says this to us irritably. I'm not sure if she's embarrassed or if she's trying to intimidate us. "I've got my hands full at Nickleby's. He should be able to hang out here for a few hours after school. I can't afford a babysitter."

"No problem, ma'am," I say.

Karl has by now joylessly descended the lamppost. She grabs him by an ear and takes him away.

Karl is using a discarded ball that he's found in the bushes and is taking shots on the rim opposite to the play. More than one person is practicing with him, jumping in to shoot on the unoccupied rim, checking the swing of the action, careful to get out of the way after a steal or a long rebound so as not to bother us while we're running up and down the court.

Games are to seven. With up to fifteen players waiting to get onto the court, we take each point seriously. The rims are unforgiving, so most of us slash to the basket, bullying our way through our check. Long debates over fouls hinder games while those on the sidelines righteously demand the resumption of play. I'm asked to mediate but my response is always the same: "I didn't see it." Often, one player grabs the basketball, says "My ball!" and then takes it to the top of the key. If the defence concedes, the game resumes grudgingly. If not, there can be trouble.

I warn Karl to get off the court more quickly — by taking an extra shot each time, he runs the risk of interrupting the game. He responds playfully, teasing me by taking his time, just missing the onslaught of our big athletic bodies running his way.

After numerous close calls, Karl takes a shot just as I leak out on the break. His ball bounces to the centre. He pounces on it. I see him in my peripheral vision as I sidestep in the other direction for the outlet. I catch the pass and turn my head down court. With forward momentum and the two-hundred-and-sixty pounds of bulk I've accumulated over the years, I drive into the little boy, my shoulders and head just missing his, my right thigh slamming into his upper torso. Karl and I hit the asphalt. I get up on my feet first. That little fuck. Blood's trickling down my leg. I pick up one of the balls and hurl it at him. The ball hits him squarely in the stomach. He doubles over and staggers off the court. It is then, blood running down my shin, staring at the boy's back as he ignobly departs, that I have a particularly unforgiving thought. After all, we can't censor all the time the way our brains operate. The thought I have is this: why can't the little man's mother shear the thicket of hair on his head? Why can't she wipe the tomatoey stain from the collar of his shirt? Why can't he brush his teeth once a day, washing the tawny drizzle from his gums and teeth?

It's Friday night and we're in the middle of an epic game. I feel guilty about yesterday, and have bought Karl a slushy. I'm waiting for him to come so I can give it to him. Only then will I be able to concentrate on my game. Adrian keeps giving me problems inside. I've got to figure out a way to get my shot off.

Off in the distance Karl's crossing the Gardiner Expressway. The setting sun doesn't provide much light so I can't see his face. As he nears the sidelines I see the smeared blood on his neck and forehead. He's picked the scabs on his knees. His hair looks matted with dirt. My lieutenant Tilley Saunders, a buddy since grade school, says, "The little freak."

"You sick sick little man, Karl," I say. "What the fuck is that in your hair? Is that shit in your hair?"

Every court has its general. At Jameson district I am this man. I decide who plays and when. My soldiers get *me* slushies from the 7-Eleven. It wasn't always like this. I once was a soldier myself. A Jamaican man, Marcus Johnson — must have been about twenty-six when I was twelve — took me under his wing in a formative period of my basketball development, and whipped my African-Canadian ass into shape and, more importantly, mentored me in the etiquette of street ball. From soldier to general was less a matter of cunning and more a matter of timing. Marcus got married, had a kid, and then another. He gradually grew fat and then one day he stopped coming. I became the next general. Admittedly, if anyone comes here and asks for the general, some of my soldiers might play dumb, you know, just to mess with me.

"Go clean yourself up, Karl. Don't come back till you're normal." I decide to keep the slushy, and I start drinking it.

Karl laughs eerily. "I want to play in the game," he says.

"Get out of here, Karl," I say. "You're freaking me out. Go get cleaned up."

He puts his head down — the weight of what I have said is far too heavy for someone his age. Shouldn't he be playing a video game? He leaves along the Expressway, the same way he came. My immediate thought is *boy, thirteen, holds up 7-Eleven with knife and is sent to Craigwood Detention Centre.* I'm a decent person. I should have taken him under my wing, I know. Marcus was good to me, after all. I'm better than this. What can I say? I'm busy at the office. I come here to let off steam. He really isn't my problem. Even if I want to help I can't. Karl is gone.

Today is Sunday, a great afternoon for a run. Adrian is dribbling the ball on the wing, which is a mistake. I'm crowding him now, forcing him to the paint where Manny, a skinny seven-footer, can hedge and double-team. Only thing is — Manny's a no show. Adrian springs off two feet and thunders down a one-handed dunk.

I grab Manny's shirt. "You've got to come with the double," I say.

At the other end I throw a pass to Tilley, but he hasn't come off the screen so the ball haplessly bounces into some nearby shrubs.

They've got possession now. Adrian's got the ball at the top of the key. It's about time that I foul him hard. I'm going to mercilessly hack his arms. Bruise him a little so that he'll think twice about dunking on me, but wait — what the fuck? He's shooting a three — an NBA three at that.

"You were late again on that double, Manny," White Rawlins says, and everyone laughs.

I grab the ball and walk across the court to where he's standing. I'm travelling, but I don't care. "I'm going to knock you silly, White Rawlins, if you keep it up."

White Rawlins doesn't like his nickname. I didn't first call him this to eliminate confusion — nobody in the neighbourhood knows of a black 'Rawlins'. I named him on an impulse and it stuck. He is at heart no different than me. We both feel a pressing need, highly ambitious at our age, to *be* NBA players — a hybrid between Gary Payton and his histrionics, though without his craziness, and Alan Iverson's cool reserve. White Rawlins has cropped hair, a sunburned nose, soppy eyes, and shorts that hang low on his hips like those worn by the disaffected street youth that I run into daily, though White Rawlins is a twenty-three-year-old FedEx driver and looks silly emulating the shorts-to-knees style. He perpetually annoys me.

"I'm on your team, James," says White Rawlins.

"You're not on any team, White Rawlins," I say.

Tilley checks the ball and then feeds it to me in the low post. I protect it with my left elbow, lower the shoulder, and pop right into Adrian's skinny frame. He's not gonna get to it this time. I knock him back, gaining some space. I reverse pivot, and with the ball high above my head I try to kiss it off the backboard. After having been dislodged from his spot in the key, Adrian is quick off his feet. His long fingers extend to the ball. He lightly taps it to his teammate, but he also hit my elbow.

"Foul," I say, with authority.

"That was clean," says White Rawlins.

I calmly give the ball to Tilley Saunders, who is standing at the top of the circle.

"You lowered your shoulder," says White Rawlins. "And besides, he got all ball. Why are *you* calling a foul?"

"Look White Rawlins, I've got a 'live and let live policy.' I tolerate your presence on this court because you add to the atmosphere. You're even amusing sometimes. But you've got to understand something. I don't want to hear you make nonsense calls from the sidelines."

"I didn't call shit. You did. I'm saying it was a non-call."

"No. You're wrong. Now look here, White Rawlins. I've let you do your thing for as long as I can remember, but I work hard at the office, and I come to this court so that I can release the toxins from my overworked body, so I don't need to hear *your* shit. Now I might tolerate your presence here, but you've got to shut your mouth while the game's on."

We lose.

In between games White Rawlins springs onto the court and tries twice to dunk a weathered volleyball. On his third attempt he squeaks in a weak two-finger dunk, hangs on the rim for a second, then falls to the ground, crosses his skinny arms and flexes, mouth open, and growls in imitation of Rasheed Wallace. This is he. He's defined what it means to be 'White Rawlins.' Only thing is — it's not natural. It's like he's driving down the express lane of Highway 401 in second gear. His effort is aggression turned inside out. Everything I know in life comes down to one principle. It's this principle that I call "Easy easy." Easy easy on the court. Easy easy with Susan and baby Anita. Easy easy with momma — more or less. Easy easy at the office. I want to impart this principle to White Rawlins, but I can't. He's got to somehow stumble onto easy easy himself. It's a journey, really. I want to give him what he needs to get there, some reassurance that I like him, but I've got my own issues — this dude, Adrian, blocking my shot and all.

So I yank White Rawlins' low-hanging shorts, which don't yield much even though they look like they'd collapse to his ankles with even the slightest provocation. "You need to have some worth," I say. "You never get into any game. You might as well get us some slushies." I grab his hand and slap a twenty-dollar bill onto it. "You can't come back without the slushies, White Rawlins." I point my finger in the direction of the 7-Eleven on the other side of the Gardiner Expressway.

White Rawlins takes a few steps away from me, and says, "I'm not buying you anything." He has no clue what to do with the cash. To leave with my money means he can't ever come back. So he walks over to me and in full view of Tilley and Manny he throws the crumpled twenty-dollar bill at my feet. I detect some soppiness that until this evening has been dormant in his eyes. I'm not heartless. Of course I pity the man. White Rawlins walks to his car, which is probably for the best. I see myself through the eyes of my soldiers — a general who mercilessly cuts the inept to strengthen the whole.

"Someone tell White Rawlins he's banished," I say, weakly. I'm walking back to the key. Two gone in two days. Oh well. "Let's go. I'm not done yet," I say to Adrian. But I don't really mean it.

White Rawlins returns, but not to the game. He's back with a curious little kid, who is wearing a shiny Toronto Raptors jersey. White Rawlins has bought a rubber basketball, and they're shooting at a rugged half-court at the other end of my park. I first bump into them in the 7-Eleven. I'm there for a hotdog. White Rawlins and the kid are filling their slushies with ice. I'm slow to identify the boy. Karl's hair has been neatly trimmed. He looks strangely out of place in the Raptors jersey. I recognize him because of his eyes — they're large and imploring and unmistakably his.

I'm curious to see what White Rawlins is doing with Karl so I follow them to the other end of my park and watch from behind a tree. I want to make sure White Rawlins is up to nothing sordid. My lieutenant, Tilley, is supervising the main court while I'm on reconnaissance.

He has Karl doing some strenuous ball handling drills. "Isaiah dribbled a basketball in line while waiting to get into a movie theatre, Karl," White Rawlins says, which is something I didn't know. The rat-a-tat of the ball bouncing from the asphalt to the tips of Karl's fingers mixes with the sound of White Rawlins' whistle. Karl doesn't complain about these drills, but a problem soon develops when White Rawlins, insisting that the best players at the college level play tough defence, has Karl chopping his feet, with his knees bent, his butt down, and with his back straight.

"I'm not doing any of this defensive stuff," Karl says. "I'm going back to the other court."

"We're going to watch the game against the Timberwolves tonight, Karl. Just a little more. You're starting to do good."

Marcus' beautiful large hand gracing my forehead. "You're really starting to come along James. I'm really proud of you. Now go on out there and shoot another two hundred." From the shoulder, like a shot put. Nothing but twine. And again that beautiful large hand on my head, confirming my sense of self-worth.

Karl has his head down, his back stooped and he's sliding sluggishly across the pebbly surface, which would be poignant if it weren't that his stance is *all* wrong. He's crossing his feet, and at times bending at the waist, which are huge no-nos. Even White Rawlins should know this.

Deer flies are taking dives at the hotdog I'm eating. This is of course irritating but what is this? Giggling? When I was Karl's age I never giggled when doing drills. White Rawlins is chucking the ball gently at Karl's back each time he passes. Karl's doing his slides lackadaisically, ignoring White Rawlins, who is trying to be funny. He glances in my direction. So does White Rawlins. Are they laughing at me? Getting even in their own way? This is all wrong.

This evening I'm point guard, though at two-hundred-and-sixty pounds I'm perhaps out of position. "Clear out," I say. "I'm gonna show this pup a thing or two about how we do things on my court." I'm dribbling so that my body is in the way, backing Adrian into the paint. I'm in no hurry at all. I fend him off with my left arm, which weighs about the same as him and I shift to the basket, scooping the ball and laying it up. But on release I let go of Adrian, who, somehow, is off his feet, trapping the ball on the backboard.

"Who the fuck do you think you are?" I say. "You're hacking me every time. My game used to be easy easy till you started fouling me."

"What are you on about, James?" Tilley says.

"What am I on about? Is it easy easy now?" I say. "No, it's fucking not easy easy. I used to be the one blocking the shots. I used to be Kevin Garnett."

"Maybe if you stopped eating hotdogs you'd block a shot or two," Adrian says.

"That's it," I say. "You leave me no choice. Get the fuck off my court."

Some of the guys groan. This is how they support me?

"I didn't know blocking shots was a crime. Are you banishing me now, James?" Adrian says.

Enough is enough. The kid has disrespected me for the last time. I can't hit him. What can I do? I can kick the ball. And so I do. I hoof the ball clear across to the other end of the park.

"I'm not getting that," I say. My eyes are buggy. That Adrian looks unfazed aggravates me all the more.

"I'll go and get it," Adrian says.

There's no fear in him at all. I get the feeling he pities me, which clearly won't do. "Just wait a second, bro'," I say. "I'm acting like an asshole. I'm gonna get the ball. Quit fucking blocking my shot though, will ya?"

Adrian laughs. Everyone else laughs a little.

But I've got to get the ball. I'm pushing things tonight. Even though it's my court I've got to be careful about how I impose my will. I don't want a mutiny or anything. So I take a short cut and run through the flowers in the garden, which causes the old surly men on the park benches to grumble. The ball is rolling toward the decrepit half court, where White Rawlins and Karl are still playing.

Three days have gone by since I banished White Rawlins and they're going strong. The July sun beats down on the playing surface. I return to the same spot behind the tree. White Rawlins is showing Karl how to do a reverse lay-up, which is okay except that White Rawlins is demonstrating this incorrectly. He's gliding under the hoop along the baseline from the left side of the court to the right, hooking the ball against the boards with his right hand, which I am sure feels right to White Rawlins, and which was endorsed by none other than Dr. J, but his form is off. It defies the laws of biomechanics. You should hook the ball with your left hand, so as to keep your body from floating away from the basket. I laugh out loud to show them I don't approve. They pretend I'm not there, which is ridiculous when you consider that I'm not hiding and my girth is twice the diameter of the maple tree.

From the court behind me, "Yo James!"

I turn around, disoriented.

"Yo James! We've only got one ball. Hurry the fuck up."

"I'll be there in a second, Tilley," I say.

Karl is now doing push-ups. His lean triceps are glistening in the sun. "Karl, come on. I need you to run with us," I say. "Come on. It's show time."

Karl looks up, as if surprised to see me. "What?" he says.

"You're going to run with Tilley, and Manny. Time to play. Enough of White Rawlins' drills."

Karl stands up and slouches his shoulders, not sure whether to come or not.

"Karl's still got two hundred shots to take, James," says White Rawlins. "We'll join you guys a little later."

This is impudent of him. "Oh, all right," I say. "You can come along as well. Just don't make me look like an idiot, White Rawlins. Little brother's coming with me whether you approve or not. And right now too. Not later. Right fucking now. Might as well hop on the bus, bro'."

Karl slowly gathers his track top. White Rawlins empties his water bottle. He complains that the water has turned warm in the heat. I grab Karl by the arm and hurry him along. I can see across the park that they're waiting for me.

When we get there, Tilley glares at White Rawlins. "What the fuck's he doing back, James? You banished him."

"It's all right. We've got a two-for-one package. Little Karl's going to play instead of me, ain't you Karl?"

"Uh huh."

"This is really exciting, right?"

"Uh huh."

The play goes up and down the court a few times. Karl doesn't touch the ball. Each time down he looks at White Rawlins, who is standing by the fence. I'm running the sidelines and yelling hysterically, "Get your man, Karl! Push him out of there, bro'! Take it strong to the hoop, Karl!" Towards the end of the game Karl slides across the key, does a v-cut and catches the ball. He squares to the basket, puts the ball on the tarmac and makes a sublime pass to Manny. His team wins by two baskets. They come to the sidelines for water, where I smother Karl, delineating the game play by play. Karl gets away from me and walks over to White Rawlins with his head down. "How do you think I played, Dean?"

"You played really good," White Rawlins says.

I notice Karl's hair is freshly cut. His tracksuit and jersey are wrinkled but clean. He looks anxious but understandably so. I'm feeling charitable toward White Rawlins so I say, "Tell you what. I've been thinking about Karl's progress. Maybe you and I can sort of co-coach him."

White Rawlins looks at the ground, shuffling his feet.

I expect my soldiers to applaud my magnanimity, but nobody seems to care.

I make eye contact. "You've done a nice job with Karl, Dean."

White Rawlins hasn't heard me. He's pushing Karl toward the court, saying, "Get in your stance, Karl!"

I yell, "Cut your man off at the baseline, Karl!"

Karl has a serious expression on his face. He bends at the knees and, with a swiftness that I haven't previously observed, he moves toward his check.

A GOOD DECISION

YESTERDAY, I RAN INTO RON, A MAN I almost ran away with forty years ago, at the grocery store. He asked me to meet him for coffee and for some inexplicable reason I agreed. This encounter has made me nervous and introspective. I've got a retired husband who deeply cares for me. I'm exhausted these days, but I still enjoy teaching. I've got one more semester at Norfolk Collegiate, and then we plan to downsize to a condo in central Toronto.

Why did I agree to meet with Ron? I don't want to revisit my youth, but lately I've been confused: a young teacher, Charlie, reminds me of Ron. And Charlie has me evaluating whether, all those years ago, I made a good decision. I feel the same as, say, a scientist, when she's studying a wolf in the wild. The classic wannabe alpha wolf is entering the cafeteria. Curly blond hair. Tall and thin. Charlie approaches us untucking his silk shirt from his faded jeans, the same way he does every day, as if he's on holiday from his students and going to enjoy his lunch even if everyone else is dull. "Those little buggers in my period B keep telling me I've been gaining weight," he says loudly. "I haven't gained any fat, have I?"

I'm amazed how young male wolves can affect others, more often than not in a positive way.

Now, let's look at Jeffrey Humphrey. Balding. Overweight. In his early thirties. He's a carbon copy of my husband, Glen, when he was that age. He's at my table, eating his pastrami sandwiches, cookies, drinking his milk and marking his papers. He breaks from this task, looks up from his quizzes, and catches Charlie lifting his shirt for Ms. Watson. She's staring at Charlie's smooth, flat stomach, a wan smile on her lips. I'm looking too. Is that so wrong? Mr. Humphrey's face contorts and from his gaping mouth loud guffaws resonate across the room.

Arzu — I only remember her name because her histrionics in my grade ten English class have left an impression — bursts into the teacher's cafeteria, as if she has every right in the world to do so.

She spots Mr. Humphrey and immediately crosses the room to our table.

Charlie, affected consternation on his face, hurries over. He puts his hands on his hips and says, "You don't belong here."

"I can come in here if I want. Nobody's going to stop me," Arzu says.

Charlie rolls up his sleeves, exposing the taut muscles in his forearms. "You do understand what we do in here when students aren't around, right?" He makes a sweeping motion with his hand to indicate the twenty or so teachers in the small room. "We take off our shoes and socks and play a gigantic game of Twister." He pauses. "But you wouldn't know about Twister, right? How old are you, Arzu? Twelve. Twelve-year-old girls have never heard of Twister."

Jeffrey Humphrey is laughing. His two chins jiggle and he pounds the table with the palm of his right hand.

Arzu giggles. "I'm sixteen. I just came in to see Mr. Humphrey about an assignment. Is that okay with you, Mr. Lyons?"

Charlie moves to the centre of the room where he has a larger audience. He's repeating what he said. The freshness of his delivery has waned, but his voice is loud enough for everyone to hear.

Mr. Humphrey, with a deep, resonant voice, says, "Didn't we play horseshoes in here just last week, Charlie?" Cookie crumbs flutter from his mouth. He gets up and quietly tells Arzu to follow him out of the cafeteria so they won't disturb anyone.

I pour oil and vinegar dressing on my taco salad. This is today's special, my favourite. Charlie, back at my table, wipes sweat from his brow, and the muscles in his face relax.

I tell him that Mr. Humphrey and Arzu have left.

He looks at me and my heart rate quickens, which is silly for a woman my age. "Oh — I wanted to, um, say something to Humphrey," he says. "Horseshoes — that was kind of funny." He looks ill at ease, but quickly recovers. "Can you believe that kid? Just comes in here like she owns the place."

Through the curls of his blond hair, his blue eyes are staring at me.

Ron took his racquet and patted me on the behind, then sat on a plastic chair near the doubles line, and spread his legs. Not bashful at all. I wanted to take my finger and lift one of his blond curls to make him uneasy in the same way that he always made me uneasy.

"You've got to work on your backhand, Marla," he said.

"Look at you. Your game is too predictable," I said. I knew that this wasn't a clever response, but Ron and I were at a point where I couldn't really do any wrong.

"I've got a fourth set in me. You don't stand a chance," he said. "But if you don't want to go another set, I'll understand." He pulled his sweaty shirt up, exposing his stomach. I could see the ripples in his abdominal muscles. There wasn't any stomach hair, which was nice.

"I know what you want," I said. "You want to play the fourth at the Spoke Club. That's not tennis, dear."

"How do you know what I want?"

"What?" I was walking away. Slowly.

"What if I want more?"

I was shaking. "You shouldn't ask." My voice was unsteady. "I can't. You know why. You've actually thought about this?"

"It sounds like you have as well."

I was crying. I hurried to the ladies' change room. I hoped he saw my tears.

It's lunch time again, and I'm at the same table with Mr. Humphrey. The special today is fish and chips, which are too greasy, so I've bought a dismal-looking tuna fish sandwich and an apple. Shirley Thompson has joined us. She looks unsettled — she's eating too quickly and talking with her mouth open. She's also spilled coffee on her blouse. I don't want to point this out. It'd just make her more self-conscious. I like Shirley a lot. She's a very diligent, conscientious teacher, if a little nervous.

"Oh my, this is just awful," Shirley says. "Just awful. Don't mind me. I've just had a terrible teaching experience. You'll never believe what happened."

"What happened, Shirley?" I say.

"Well, you know how in Canadian history we teach World War Two? I wanted to show some footage of the war so, you know, my students could see what war is all about. Anyway, someone recommended the movie *Saving Private Ryan*. Oh — I really wish I hadn't shown that film. Do you know how graphic it is? In the first ten minutes all you see is men getting killed. Someone's hand gets shot off. I mean, he actually picks it up from the beach. Some of my students started to laugh because it is so . . . awful. Oh, their parents will think I'm such an awful person."

From out of nowhere, Charlie is at our table. His arm is around her. "Show them *The Sound of Music*. A classic World War Two movie. This will put them in better spirits. They'll forget all about the horrific violence."

He winks at us. There's something contradictory about Charlie: his innate curiosity, his playfulness, and his need to turn every discussion into mockery.

"What?" Shirley says.

"Your students could sing along to the songs," he says.

She ignores him. "Oh — I'm such an awful person. What am I going to do tomorrow?"

Charlie shuffles a deck of cards in his long slender fingers. Every few seconds he plucks cards from the top, and whips them back inside the deck. "No one gets any body parts blown off in *The Sound of Music*."

"Show them another video?" she says. "Why?"

Mr. Humphrey's large hand grabs Shirley's shoulder and pulls her gently away from Charlie. "You don't want to show another movie, Shirley." He says this dismissively. "The best thing you can do tomorrow is to be you."

Shirley smiles and says, "Oh thank you, Jeffrey. You're so nice. I still can't help feeling terrible about what happened today."

Mr. Humphrey wipes his red nose with his sleeve. "What I mean is — you are an extremely warm teacher. You really care. What can you do tomorrow? I think the most important thing you can do for your students is to be yourself. You give them so much every day. You're probably not even aware how much you do for your students."

"Oh — that's so nice," Shirley says.

Charlie looks embarrassed by Jeffrey's lovely remarks. "You guys should probably embrace," he says, then goes back to his table. When he picks up his sandwich, his face betrays irritation, but only for a second.

On my way out of the cafeteria, I walk over to his table. "Jeffrey wasn't trying to upstage you, Charlie," I say.

"You don't understand. Really, you don't. Shirley needs to be herself. You need to be yourself. Mr. Humphrey needs to be himself. This may surprise you but what I want is to *be* Jeffrey Humphrey." He says this absentmindedly. "Does this surprise you?"

"You're fine just the way you are, Charlie," I say.

"Do you think Jeffrey and I will ever be chums?"

I look over at Jeffrey — his eyes are too close together and his skin is dry and pink.

Glen was crying, his large body hunched over, his bald head in his hands. He lifted the bottom of his shirt to wipe his eyes. This made it more difficult for me to do what I had to do. I saw the tangle of black, curly hairs on his stomach. His belly button jiggled as he shook with grief. The sight of this made me feel worse. I felt vain and shallow and totally alone in the world. I didn't deserve to be loved.

"I will always take you back," Glen said. "Even if you go out with someone else and it doesn't work out. I'll take you back. I don't care."

"There's no one else." I began to cry. Not because I didn't love him. I did. But because he'd just inadvertently referred to the truth. Or part of the truth. I wasn't sure.

I tried to hug him. He warded me off with his big, meaty hand and said, "I can't right now." His eyes were steady and dignified. "I'm sorry. I want to be alone."

I didn't. I wanted to stay with him. I wished he'd say something so angry that it would make this easier.

I'm enjoying the special today, lasagna with a garden salad and milk. Mike Fryer and Julian Middleton, both science teachers, are at the next table, huddled around Charlie. "There's nothing more important than having a bit of fun in class, right? Nothing worse than a dull class," Charlie says. "During a work period, just when the kids are completely silent, I walk around and make sure they're on task. I stop beside one of the shyer students, just like this." Charlie squats next to Arnie Wilson, an older geography teacher, and lowers his mouth to his ear. "I say, 'What was that, Shu Dong?' When Shu Dong says nothing, I say, 'That's a great idea, Shu Dong.' One of the rowdier kids asks me what's a great idea. I say, 'Shu Dong just brought something to my attention. Apparently, we haven't had much homework over the last few days. Shu Dong loves to study. He's just asked me to assign an extra reading assignment for everyone tonight. This isn't my idea.

It's Shu Dong's.' The kids in class boo Shu Dong, who is truly mortified by now. It's all in good fun."

Arnie Wilson pulls his chair back, so that he's away from Charlie. He's smiling though.

"Kids need comic relief," Charlie continues. "This is most important. If not, what tedium. I can't stand a boring class."

A deep voice interrupts Charlie. "Get them to believe in themselves."

Everyone turns to see who has spoken.

"What?" Charlie says.

"I differ in opinion," Mr. Humphrey says. "I think a vital part of my job is getting students to believe in themselves." He rubs his nose with his index finger.

"What do you mean?" Charlie says. His cheeks are suddenly pale. He turns away. Nobody notices except me, and within two or three seconds he has recovered.

"My job as a teacher," Mr. Humphrey says, "is to get my students to believe in themselves. The students at this school are all wonderful people, and they need to know this." I look closely at Mr. Humphrey. He's chewing slowly, a concerned look on his face that isn't at all self-righteous.

Charlie wants to say something. This impulse dies and he quietly sighs.

Everyone smiles politely.

After I eat, I still have twenty minutes before next class. I tuck my arm under Charlie's arm, and gently pull him out of his seat. I whisk him to a corner of the room. "Mr. Humphrey wasn't trying to make you look bad. He was merely saying something that he really believed. He wasn't trying to contradict you in any way. He's a nice guy if you get to know him."

"I know he's a nice guy. I know what he's all about. I don't think that he really *understands* me, though."

"Really?"

"There is this one project," Charlie says, "that I created in my grade eleven English class. I get the kids to read their own poetry. I bring in candles and dim the lights. I think he'd like it."

We both look at Mr. Humphrey, who is sitting at the other end of the room, marking his papers, eating his pastrami sandwich and scratching his sideburns.

"Go on — why don't you tell him?"

"What if he doesn't like me?" Charlie laughs nervously.

"He'll like you. Go over there. He won't hurt you."

"All right."

Charlie crosses the room (I'm reminded of Peter, my grandson, approaching another boy on his first day of kindergarten). Mr Humphrey is deeply concentrating on what he's marking. For a moment I'm worried that he might dismiss Charlie, or even worse might react to him with irritation. A few, maybe three, seconds pass. Mr. Humphrey finally glances up, his face breaking into a smile. He asks Charlie to sit with him and right away the two are having an intimate conversation. Mr. Humphrey's head nods vigorously from time to time. Ms. Thompson is talking to me, so I'm distracted, but when the bell rings and it's time to get to class, I'm privy to part of their conversation.

"The problem in this place is that nobody really *believes* in themselves," Charlie says.

Mr. Humphrey, his voice flat and solemn, says, "You know what my problem is — you don't take me seriously. You always poke fun at me."

There's an uncomfortable silence and Charlie looks distraught.

Mr. Humphrey gently pokes him in the ribs. Deep from his diaphragm erupts a bellow, surprising at first, but it allows Charlie and me to breathe relief.

Charlie laughs too and I'm really quite astonished — not by his laughter but by something else. There is a puppy-dog, eager-to-please expression on his face.

I meet Ron at the coffee shop. He's sitting at a table. I walk over, my hand patting down an unwieldy clump of grey hair. He's still sort of nice-looking, but his features have bloated and he's gained weight around his stomach. I tell him about my youngest daughter — how she's studying fine art at Queen's. He interrupts me to remind me again about how I was lucky to beat him at tennis all those years ago.

"Are you still playing?" he says. He strokes my arm, which gives me the willies. He has a wayward look in his eyes that suggests he wants to rekindle some of the same feelings that we had for each other, but I don't want this. I suppose Ron would always be trying to impress me, or even worse, trying not to impress me — too much effort, I now understand.

"Glen is fine," I say, unsolicited, "He's been taking wood-working classes for about a decade. I've relied on him. He's very insightful. I've come to learn that I'm an anxious person, which is okay because Glen listens to my worries. He sits in his big old armchair and listens to every word that I say. It's been nice."

I've said too much, and I worry for an instant that Ron thinks that I'm a foolish old woman. He probably isn't thinking this, though. His eyes are watery.

GREEN JERSEYS

IT IS MONDAY, JUNE 10, A COOL morning. There's just one more week of school. I'm fifty years old and I'm flashing cards, homemade, blue ink on white Bristol board, at Bobby Fenner, who has his head in his arms. Tiny red pimples dot his cheeks.

Soup Kitchen.

"What's the significance of this, Bobby?" My deep voice resonates off the blackboards.

"I don't know," he says lethargically.

"Hey Bobby, cheer up," I say, my teeth clenched, rubbing my knuckles against the top of his greasy blond head to motivate him.

"Don't do that," he says. "Oh — I don't know. That's where people got free food because they were hungry."

"That's right, Bobby. How about this one?" *Bennett Buggy.*

"They didn't have enough gas, so they hooked their cars up to horses."

"Bingo, Bobby. Five for five." The room is boisterous. Kids are turned around in their desks, squirming. Tanya Simmons is painting her chipped nails an awful shade of pink. Sara Roberts is looking in a mirror, covering her acne with blush. These kids are unruly. I'm going to have to rein them in one of these days. I'm only the educational assistant in this class. Stan Wakefield is the actual teacher, but he doesn't have authority, and he's not here now because he's taken Lee Hendry down to the office for throwing gum at Tanya.

"That's enough for today, Bobby." I turn to Simon Winters, the other kid that I help. We're playing chess. Just for fun. I'm about to advance my bishop to b3, pressuring Simon to castle. Simon, cerebral for his age, indifferent to history in general, but nevertheless soaking up the review lessons on CCF social programs and the Great Depression, says, "We're not going to have enough time to finish, Mr. Petropolous."

"There's no need to panic, Simon." My Philidor defence is overwhelming him. "It won't take me long now." Out of the corner of my eye, I see Henry's pink flesh, like Easter ham, fill the tiny window in the door. His two pea-sized eyes are staring at me. He's an educational assistant as well. We are of the same ilk, yet I feel antagonistic toward him in the same way that people are ashamed of their family. He's also the wrestling coach, but his kids lose all their matches. For which I fault him entirely. I get up and open the door.

"I want to see Riley for a minute, Gus."

I turn. Riley, a grotesquely strong boy, his thick torso and beard making him look at least twenty-two, is rising from his desk. "Have a seat, Riley." I say to Henry, "Riley's busy. Can he see you at lunch?"

Henry takes a step. His protruding belly, expanding daily from eating *mangia* food, bumps me. My hands grip both sides of the doorframe.

"Actually, do you mind if I ask the teacher about this, Gus?"

"I *am* a teacher, Henry." I say. "So are you."

He's looking over my right shoulder for Stan. "Whatever, Gus," he says. "Tell Riley I want to see him after class."

Principal Phillips hired me as a special education assistant ten months ago, at the end of August. It hasn't been a great year.

At lunchtime I usually buy a tuna sandwich and an apple from the cafeteria and eat on the front steps, gazing at the athletic field. When I'm done, I read *Maclean's Magazine* or go for a walk on Danforth Avenue. I often come back to class with my pants wrinkled and dusty. After he hired me, Principal Phillips tried to convince me to eat in the staff room with everyone else. Apparently, they have interesting conversations. An absurdly close-knit bunch, if you ask me. I told him I went outside because of the nice weather. By late October it was cold and blustery, yet I still stayed away from the staff room. At lunch I moved to the auditorium where students aren't allowed. Kids peered in through the windows and watched me sitting in the vast place, silently eating and reading my magazine. I'm glad to be outside again. Today Bobby sits beside me. I tell him to piss off — not in these words exactly. I spend enough time with him in the classroom.

It's Tuesday, four more days till summer break. I've decided to use the staff room at lunch to revise my résumé. Peter, my *filo* from Starlight Billiards, read in the *Toronto Star* that there's a demand for tool-and-die makers and gave me the information last night. That is what I'm thinking about, tool-and-die. I'm steadfastly and proudly wearing my green Panathinaikos football jersey. After all, we beat Olympiakos in the semi-finals last night. Henry walks in, stares at my jersey. "I like your getup, Gus. You forgot your cleats though, buddy."

Buddy? He's sitting in his armchair, which was left in storage after a school play, until he moved it to the staff room.

That he brought it here himself is his justification for removing anyone ignorant enough to sit in it. Apparently an unknowing student teacher sat in it one morning in September. Henry came up from behind and picked him up by his armpits and, without explanation, dumped him onto another chair.

I don't like to talk much so I sit, revising my résumé, though not really able to concentrate. Henry gets up to get a cola. I take my *souvlaki* and my tomato juice across the staff room and plop my ass down. In *his* armchair.

My *souvlaki* is leftovers from yesterday's victory dinner. A little of the *tsatziki* spurts from the sandwich and lands on my collar. I wipe it up. I'm preparing myself. Eyes partially closed, tensing, then relaxing, first my legs, next my arms. Aware but not too aware, if you know what I mean. I imagine myself clamping down, wriggling, and elbowing fat Henry in the ribs. Principal Phillips enters the room and is surprised to see me. He whispers something to Ian, a drama teacher, and leaves. I guess he can't take the tension. Henry's by the pop machine, staring at me, brooding. A cool cucumber. He sits down with Nancy and Gwen and says, "Have you read Grisham's latest?"

Another guy, Enright, tall but with a skinny upper body, makes eye contact with Henry. "So why aren't you in your seat, Henry?" he says.

"Guess I've been kicked out," Henry says.

Enright laughs. It's clear he sympathizes with Henry.

I slowly lick the *tsatziki* off the pita, and drink my tomato juice. People turn the pages of the *Toronto Star*, this crinkling the only sound in the room. Eventually, Mrs. Sherman sits down beside me. "How have you been these days, Gus?" she says.

"Just great," I say. "Thanks for asking." She should ask
Henry how he's doing. He's the one she should be concerned
about. I want to tell her that the teachers at Woodbine
Collegiate are strange. Why is everyone so interested in each
other's business? I'm licking my fingers. There isn't much else
to do. "Sorry, I'm not much into chitchat today, Mrs. Sherman."
I look away. Mrs. Sherman has long, slender legs — she's a
genuine *oraia*.

"Thanks for doing such a nice job in my class, Gus," she
says.

I don't know why this irks me, but it does. "The sub did
nothing. I'd like you to come in and control your kids while
you're away sick."

"Oh, that makes sense," Henry says.

Some of the *mangias* are laughing. Out loud. So I leave.
Why do I have to put up with this abuse? Tool-and-die?
Sounds nice. The kids at this school ridicule my accent and
tease me because I'm hairy. I treat the little *zouzounia* like
flies: I am a cow ignoring flies that land on its nose. Bobby
Fenner especially. When he tags along, he clips my ankles
from behind. I like to get away from him and chat with kids
who aren't looking for my attention. Bobby is slow. He poked
my stomach and danced around me for over three months
before figuring out that I wasn't interested in his games.

But I give Bobby attention this day, the day of my pseudo-
confrontation with Henry. He's alone in the south wing.
"How's the tennis team, Bobby?"

"It's great, Gus. How's the mafia?" And then, like a puppy,
he's at my heels. "Just joking, Gus. I mean Mr. P. Tennis is
great. I'll see you in history."

"It starts in two minutes, Bobby." I say. "Nobody will bother me at the tool-and-die." He doesn't hear me because he's running to class.

Desks dragged on the tile floor make a scraping noise. Mr. Wakefield is addressing the students. He's short with wispy red hair, and has a big nose and red moustache. He's usually earnest and idealistic around our students, like a college professor. He delivers his lectures in a monotone voice, but sometimes after class he surprises me by making lustful comments about the girls in grade twelve, entirely out of character, but erasing any barrier between teacher and assistant. Today his voice is soft, so soft that I can't hear him above the din. "What'd he just say, Bobby?"

Bobby is chewing on his arm, so his words are muffled. "He said we got to get it in by the end of class."

Marcia looks inside her duffle bag, finds a ticket from the Killers concert, and shows it to Tanya, holding it with two fingers, but Tanya doesn't take it because she's applying eyeliner. Tom is staring at Tanya's *stithoi*. I don't really blame the young *mangia*. Lee sticks some gum under his desk, in full view of everyone. He picks up his *Canada in the Twentieth Century* scrapbook and tosses it on Mr. Wakefield's desk. Tom does the same, as does Marcia, and Tanya. The rest follow suit. 2:45. Thirty-five minutes left. Nothing's been accomplished, and only one forlorn book remains on a desk. Bobby's. He's trying to put it away, but is having a difficult time because my hairy thumb is pinning it on his desk.

"I'm going to have a word with these kids, Bobby," I say.

"Don't. Please don't," says Bobby.

I stand up and flick the lights on and off four times. "If you little *zouzounia* don't finish your assignments, you're staying after the bell. I've got my hand on the door knob and am not letting go until I've checked everything." My knuckles are turning red. I won't let go for the Bishop of the Athens Chancery. "I'm going to track you *zouzounia* down if you try and hand in something subpar. I've got a whole box of extra-credit assignments: word searches, crosswords, math worksheets. And I'm going to make you do them if you haven't handed in quality work."

Bobby looks mortified. Mr. Wakefield does as well. He's unwilling to look in my direction.

Kids whisper to each other, then everything is quiet. It is like the phony war before the Battle of Britain (stuff we're going to review tomorrow). It's like this for a very, very long time. Wasted time.

The bell rings to signal the end of the day.

"You can't keep us in here," says Tanya.

"Just watch me," I say, through clenched teeth. These are the words of Pierre Trudeau, the only Canadian prime minister that I respect.

"You're going to need your mafia friends to back you up," says Tom Riddley.

I've only been in Canada for five years. My English still isn't great. They believe I'm an ignorant man. They can't leap into the awareness that, even though I don't say much and even though I pronounce things incorrectly, there's an acute consciousness on this side of my thick eyebrows. I speak two languages. I've read Plato and the Greek tragedies. I *understand* them.

"I don't *need* anybody," I say. My hand is sweating and I worry about my grip on the doorknob.

Lee Hendry crosses the room. I smell his cheap aftershave. He sticks his hand mutinously in the direction of the doorknob, and his fingers make fleeting contact with mine.

I slap them away. He winces in pain, but doesn't show this to the rest of the class. He goes back to his seat and schemes with his dithering thugs. They distract me so I'm late to see the next wave of attack, led by none other than Mr. Wakefield himself, flanked by Marcia and Tanya. "Can I talk to you for a second, Gus?" he says.

"You can talk to me, Mr. Wakefield, but I'm not letting go of my grip on this door. Not until they've done the assignment you handed out."

"Tanya needs to get on the 3:45 GO Train to see her dad in Mississauga. She can't miss this train. Do you think we could let her out into the world? Maybe negotiate everyone else's release after?" Mr. Wakefield says this with such concern for Tanya that my Mediterranean heart warms to him. Tanya is standing beside both of us now, tears streaking her mascara.

"I'll let her out, Mr. Wakefield, on one condition," I say.

Tanya's face breaks into a smile.

"What's that, Gus?" he says.

"She does her assignment."

Mr. Wakefield walks back to his desk with his head down. I feel bad for him. It isn't his fault he can't control his class.

The peevish kids finally get to it and ten minutes later, at 3:40, they throw their uninspired, but completed assignments on Mr. Wakefield's desk.

I heroically open the door. "You've got no one to blame but yourselves."

They stream past me, jeering, contempt in their eyes. There are three people left in the room: Mr. Wakefield, Bobby and me. Bobby has tears in his eyes. He's probably feeling responsible for my behaviour and is angry, rightly so. "I'm sorry if I embarrassed you, Bobby," I say.

He's crying more openly now, which makes me uncomfortable. "I'm so stupid," he says.

"What do you mean, Bobby?"

"I'm so stupid. Forget about it." He packs up his books.

"You're not stupid, Bobby," I say. "Not at all. Why would you say something like that?" I rub his forehead with my knuckles, which has cheered him up in the past, but which now makes him lurch away from me.

"I couldn't do the work," says Bobby. "You were up at the front and I couldn't do it. I looked at the pages, but without help I couldn't do anything."

"Look, Bobby — *you* normally are the one helping *me* with the work." This lie only makes his nose runnier, and speeds up his packing. I grab him by the belt of his trousers and sit him down. "Bobby, you are *not* stupid. You can do this assignment by yourself. All you need is a shove in the right direction. Watch, I'll show you." I open the scrapbook to the Table of Contents. "First question: World War II. What was the wartime consumption of meat per capita by Canadians? Where are we going to find this?" I say.

"I don't know."

I skim my index finger down the table. "Is it this, Hitler and his Storm troopers?" "No." "Is it this, Enlistment of forces?" "No." "How about this, Bobby — is it, Housewives and Duty?" "Well, maybe," he says. "What page is that on?" "It's on page 26." I turn to that page.

"Five pounds," he says.

"Bingo, Bobby. You're the man."

We finish. He looks embarrassed — perhaps by his earlier fit of crying, so I say, "You're going to ace the exam on Friday, Bobby."

He says, "Thanks, Mr. Petropolous," and leaves.

Mr. Wakefield has been quietly watching Bobby and me. When I get up to leave he averts his gaze in order to examine something on his desk.

"Are you going to the pool hall for a pint, Stan?" I say.

"We'll see," he says. "See you tomorrow, Gus."

Mr. Wakefield is a stand-up guy. During the entire standoff at the door, he had my back. He went from desk to desk, controlling the kids one by one while I protected the front. Anyone looking in on our class would have seen us working in tandem. He's one of the nicest *mangias* I've ever met. Before our first class in September he pulled me aside in the hallway. He said, "Listen Gus, when we're in the classroom together we're a team. I don't believe in labels. As far as I'm concerned we're *both* teachers. There's no hierarchy here."

I looked him in the eyes. "Thanks Stan. That means a lot to me."

It is Wednesday. I'm feeling exuberant. I won two hundred dollars from Peter at the Starlight last night. Easily, in fact. Peter was tipsy when I arrived, and I was up after the first improbable break. This afternoon the kids are wary of me. I sense it. I flick the lights a few times and everyone groans. "Just joking," I say.

Mr. Wakefield says, "Can I talk to you for a minute, Gus?" I confer with him in the hallway. He looks uneasy. "About yesterday," he says. "Maybe I should take care of classroom discipline. There are just a few more days till the end of the semester. Is this okay with you?"

"I was a little out of line yesterday," I say.

He looks relieved. "Don't get me wrong, Gus," he says. "We're still a team. You teach. I teach. We support each other, right?"

"You bet, Stan," I say.

Mr. Wakefield gives his lecture, droning on about victory bonds, conscription of farmers from Owen Sound, about Nazi atrocities and about how wives needed to persuade their cowardly husbands to join the fighting. Blah. Blah. Blah. Part of the curriculum sure, but he's completely forgotten to include a major part of the story.

"Please forgive me, Mr. Wakefield." I'm standing, and at least for me it seems as if no time has passed since yesterday. "We've only got thirty more minutes and tomorrow we're reviewing the baby boom and suburban life in the 50s."

"That's right. So?" says Mr. Wakefield, looking bewildered.

"Forgive me but I think you forgot to talk about how Greece dealt the first victory for the allies by resisting the initial attempts of the Italian invasion and pushing Mussolini back into Albania. You see, kids, Hitler was forced to send troops and delay the invasion of the Soviet Union by six weeks. This was the turning point of the war. The German invasion was disastrous as a result of the cold Russian winter. The Germans also met fierce Greek resistance on the island of Crete. German paratroopers suffered almost seven thousand casualties. These heavy losses eliminated the option of a massive airborne invasion of the Soviet Union and further expansion in the Mediterranean, saving Malta, Gibraltar, Cyprus, and the Suez Canal. The Greeks hung in tough and if it wasn't for them . . . "

The bell rings. Having day-dreamed away my stirring lecture, the kids are packing up their books. "Next time you should take some notes," I say.

Today is Thursday. I stick my head into Principal Phillips's office. "Hi, Ron. Just two more days."

He's busy doing paperwork. He lifts his head. "Oh hi, Gus. I didn't see you there."

I walk through his sparsely furnished office to his washroom. I try to be quick. The staff washrooms are disgusting. There's toilet paper and potpourri in here and there aren't any hairs on the rim of the bowl. I don't know how it is this clean. Maybe he does it himself.

Principal Phillips knocks on the door after about twenty minutes and says, "When you're done in there, Gus, could I talk to you for a moment?" I don't answer him because I'm squeezing one out and I want him to go away — so he won't hear the worst of it.

I look around for some air freshener but can't find any. I leave the washroom and walk over to his desk, where he's reading a document. He has a stern look that has me guessing. When he looks up at me, though, he smiles tenderly. "Mr. Wakefield has given you a glowing report, Gus," he says. "He says you're doing a great job with Bobby Fenner."

"Stan's doing a great job too," I say. "I can't take all the credit." I laugh. He laughs too.

"Stan and I have been talking about you lately. If you're interested, there's an opportunity for you to attend teacher's college, Gus. The University of Maine needs Canadian students next semester. The paper work can be filled out online. I've set up a phone interview with the Dean of the Faculty of Education. It was my idea, actually. You might not end up back with us, but you'll be a teacher. It's a rewarding job."

"Are you sure this is a good idea?" I say.

"Of course. You'll have to officially resign as an educational assistant, but you can come back and visit. I think this is the best thing for everyone, Gus."

"Who's going to be the ed. assistant in Stan — in Mr. Wakefield's class? Who's going to control the little . . . ?" I almost say, "*zouzounia*", but say, "troublemakers?"

"Oh, I don't know. Maybe I can free up Henry for your class."

"Henry. The students won't like that."

"Oh well, they'll have to get used to it. It's not really your concern, though. I mean, you'll be at teacher's college." Phillips smiles. "We'll all miss you, Gus. But you're going to a better place. Believe me — you'll enjoy the control you'll have as a teacher."

"I suppose."

"Okay, Gus. I'll set up a phone interview for you tomorrow. You can call from here. I can also help you with the online forms."

"Okay. Thanks, I guess."

"Big game tonight, Gus." He's smiling.

"I know."

"Good luck. Oh and Gus, make sure you come to the staff room tomorrow at lunch. You're the only staff member leaving Woodbine and we've got sort of a special event planned for you."

I rack the balls. I'm down about a hundred and fifty dollars to Peter. The Starlight is packed with my friends. Mostly Greeks, but a few Italians and *mangias*. We're all watching the big screen — Panaithinakos is playing AEK for the Greek Cup. The biggest game of the decade, but for some reason my eyes keep wandering away from the set. Who is going to take care of Bobby?

I spill some beer on my green jersey. I'm getting drunk tonight. But it's not really a celebration. I have a bad feeling that I attribute to worry. After all, my team might lose.

Alexander Tziolis breaks free from the AEK defender. He's miraculously on side. He stuffs the ball past the keeper. A beautiful goal. Was it, though? Did I see this goal or not? Do I have to go to teacher's college? I can be a teacher in Wakefield's class. I don't have to go to a university for that, right?

It's 2:30 at night and I'm drunk, staring at the television set. I'm angry at Principal Phillips, I think. I don't know exactly why. We're not jumping up and down anymore. Not that I did much of this. In the middle of the frenzied hoopla I tried talking to Peter about my feelings — about what I want to do with my life — but he didn't want any part of it. Alexander Tziolis is standing on the mostly-deserted pitch. A reporter from Hellenic Radio and Television is interviewing him. Alexander Tziolis is saying, "I'll never leave. I'll never leave."

"What do I do, Alexander?" I ask. I'm crying a little.

"Go home, Gus," says the bartender.

"Alexander Tziolis is talking to me," I yell. "The volume on the set is too low. Turn it up!" But I'm too drunk to sort anything out anyway.

It's Friday, the last day of school, and they're patiently waiting for me. I'm hung-over as all hell, but my brain is working. I peek inside the shabbily furnished staff room. Newspapers and old magazines are scattered everywhere. This place could stand some improvements. Maybe some new curtains. I'm thinking a ping-pong table or a pool table might make a nice addition. They're all wearing these green football jerseys. It's funny, actually. The shirts have numbers hastily taped to their backs. Some of these numbers are starting to peel. They have the same feature drawn on their faces: a thick, black moustache. This is their way of having some fun. A going-away party. Though I don't want to go anywhere. They wouldn't go to all this trouble if they didn't like me. This makes it an easy decision.

I'm not wearing my green jersey. It's got puke and beer on it. When I got up this morning I was too hung-over to clean it. Sorry to disappoint. I've got to put on a game face, smile, mingle, and eat some of their *mangia*-cake and evaluate my options.

I walk into the packed room. Everyone's patting me on the back. Henry is wearing a jersey that is tight on him. What position does he think he's playing? Stan's arm wraps around my large back.

"I've got an important announcement to make," I say.

We should, I am now thinking, have a potluck lunch every month. I'd like to start up a chess club too. What I'd really like — I'd really like to take responsibility over all educational assistants. Henry won't like it much, but he's going to have to put up with it. He might eventually like me as a boss, since I will lobby for educational assistants to have much more autonomy. Maybe we can deliver some of the class lectures. I'm thinking fifty-fifty. Otherwise we get bored, right? How about a discipline room? If the little *zouzounia* disrupt class, we'll send them to that room. Teachers can man it on their prep time. I'm also thinking Principal Phillip's time is up. Stan would make a much better principal. I want to run these ideas by my new *filos*. Except maybe the bit about the treasonous

Phillips. I'll work secretly on that next year. Despite my aching head, I feel pretty good. "I've changed my mind . . . "

"We're going to miss you, Gus," says someone from the back.

"I know, but just listen. I've got these plans. You don't understand . . . " And as I'm saying this I can feel Stan's arm slacken. Phillips is saying, "Can we discuss this in private, Gus?" But I forge ahead. "Listen, everyone, we've got to start advocating for ourselves, right?"

MAYBE YOU SHOULD GET BACK THERE

CHRIS AND I ARE LYING ACROSS FROM each other on a sofa and loveseat watching the Utah Jazz and the Los Angeles Lakers. I have a lot on my mind. We're watching cable television that for the last four months I and I alone have paid for. Chris actually tidied this evening, but this was only the first time since he moved in with Nadia and me. He never cleaned when we were living in the same dorm room together as frosh at the University of Toronto and I wish he hadn't tonight — cleaned, that is. That he's picked up the sports section, lightly dusted the television and lackadaisically vacuumed around the coffee table, does little to change my opinion of him — that he's not to be trusted.

Strictly speaking, his general dereliction of and sudden interest in household chores isn't really what's troubling me.

"Get the ball to Shaq," Chris says. His wiry arms are flexed at right angles in front of his chest, and his wispy blond bangs are stuck to his forehead. "Shaq's not getting any touches."

I find it strange that he's so involved. Chris (all 5' 7 inches of him) has never taken part in a formal game of basketball. It should be me who is shouting at the TV. Another thing — I've been trying to determine just how much better-looking Chris is than me. Empirically there's no doubt. I'm not beating myself up unnecessarily. I'm sure women in China, women in Bangladesh, and women from tribes in sub-Saharan Africa would all agree. To what degree though? This is what I'm sorting out. His eyes are dark and soft, like a calf's. His sideburns, though unkempt, are like a blond aureole framing an ethereal-looking face. Wait a second. I don't think I've ever noticed this. From this angle on the sofa, his lips look demonstrably thin. I need to see how thin my own lips are so I go to the kitchen, where there is a mirror to look at my reflection. I pucker my mouth.

"Why are you making that face?" Nadia says.

"I burned my mouth eating pizza last night. I want to see the damage."

"Let me see."

"It's all right. My mouth's okay. I think my lips may be a little more supple than usual. What do you think?"

"Your lips are nice," Nadia says.

"There isn't one black spectator in that whole arena," Chris says from the other room.

Nadia, wiping her hands on her apron, says, "What did you say, Chris?"

She walks toward the kitchen door, but I cut her off. "He just said that there aren't any black people at the game in Utah. That's all."

She sits on the sofa. I sit next to her. "What did you say?" she says.

"There aren't any black spectators watching the Jazz," Chris says. "In fact, there isn't one visible minority in that entire arena."

Nadia laughs. "That's because they're all Mormon," she says. "The Mormon church doesn't invite ethnic minorities into their congregation."

"There are more black guys on the court right now," Chris says, "than there are in all of Salt Lake City."

"Utah's kind of a funny place. Did you know that there's a fundamentalist sect of Mormonism in Utah that practices polygamy?" Nadia says.

Chris readjusts his body so that he's resting his head on the loveseat cushion. His legs extend to a coffee table. "I could really go for that. Two or three wives might not even be sufficient. They could take shifts."

"Why should you get two wives?" She looks at the television screen. "I think you should share a woman with another man. You'd be okay with that, right Chris?"

"It's not me you have to worry about. You'd better ask Max."

Nadia giggles.

"Yeah, that'd be fine with me." I'm stroking her calves with my right hand. "I have that restaurant booked for your birthday next Friday. You're going to have to get off before seven o'clock."

"Okay. Remind me on Thursday." She turns to Chris. "So women can have two husbands, right Chris? And you think the world would be absolutely okay with that?"

"I suppose. Have three if you want. However many you want, Nadia," he says. He's now moved to the floor with his back against the loveseat. His right hand is conspicuously inside his belt. He's scratching, not his genitals, but close enough to that region. What bugs me is that Nadia can see this as well. If he knew her at all, he'd understand that she thinks this kind of behaviour is vulgar. I should know. She's been my live-in girlfriend for the last four years.

"Don't your nuts get sweaty if your fingers are on them all the time?" I say.

Chris withdraws his hand and struggles upright. "It's sort of an ugly habit of mine."

Nadia is breathing shallowly.

"Did you hear that, Nadia? I just asked Chris if he had sweaty nuts because he's always scratching them."

Nadia smiles for a moment too long and says, "It doesn't bother me."

"It doesn't bother me either," I say. "I just think it is sort of funny. That's all."

My thoughts unfurl four years to Camp Skyhawk. Petey, Jamie, Nadia and I were all counsellors. We were eighteen. Nadia always wore those sweatpants that she managed to keep clean even though we'd been on the docks, her hair tied in pigtails. During late night pickup games she and her friends lay in the wicker chairs and pretended not to watch us. Jamie was also in love with Nadia. In late night pickup games Jamie dunked often, hanging on the rim, knees brushing against the mesh, but to no advantage because, well, because of me. I guarded him, and at least slowed him down, keeping my chest in front of his hips and pushing him in different directions. On offense, not trying too hard, I took my man back door, faked up and under, shoulders square, feet square, ball with just enough back spin to tease the front of the rim and fall through, then hustling back on defence to show that I was serious.

I haven't seen my buddy, Petey, in three years. I am too lethargic to call him out of the blue. I also don't want to burden him. It's a shame, though, Petey. You know me, the real me that is — not the person who lives in this house, working at TD Canada Trust, just hanging on, thinking these depressing thoughts. Remember Skyhawk, Petey?

How could I forget? That was the best summer of my life.

Jamie was always challenging Nadia to one-on-one games, but it was kid's stuff really because at the tuck shop I walked up to her like it was the most natural thing in the world and said, "So what's R.H. Henry High School like anyway?" Know what I remember? Nadia and me on the docks towelling off. It was late. We had to hurry back to our cabins. Jamie cut us off on the path and said, "Can't touch the rim can you, Max?" I smiled at him. Why would I care? Nadia liked me. I had nothing to worry about. We hadn't even kissed yet, hadn't even held hands for that matter, but we were already a couple. There was nothing was extraordinary about this. It was an unassailable fact.

You were the perfect couple.

Thanks for saying that Petey.

Nadia gets up from the sofa and answers the phone. She takes the cordless into the other room, her voice suddenly sounding grave. She comes back, white-faced. "My grandfather just had a heart attack." She absent-mindedly pitches the phone, which clatters on the coffee table. "Oh God, I've got to get back there. I've got to see him. My poor grandmother. Oh God, my mom. I can't even imagine what she's going through."

A brief interlude affords me some time to articulate in my head some soothing words for her, but I've taken too long.

"My friend's dad has a heart condition," Chris says. "A serious one. He had a heart attack just three years ago and he's fine now. As long as they get your grandfather to the hospital he'll be okay."

"He's been in the hospital for about three hours and the doctors say he's going to be all right, but . . . " Nadia holds back tears. "I can't go back. I don't have the money and I'm going there in March anyway. That should be okay, right?"

"Of course it is, honey." I walk over and put my arm around Nadia, who in turn hugs me. After a few seconds she asks Chris if his friend's father has had any more problems.

"No, not at all. He's doing great. He walked a half marathon last month. The doctor has him eating vegetables and he can still drink his Beefeater Gin. He had a pacemaker sewn in his chest that regulates the beating of his heart. It feels uncomfortable but my friend says his dad has gotten used to it and now it's like it is not even there."

Do you hear this dude, Petey? God, he is shallow. How cliché. His friend's father had a heart attack three years ago and is okay. Nadia's not even listening to what he's saying.

You're right, Max. Not really playing by the rules, is he? Hitting on another guy's girl and all.

"You do remember that we're going to Palermo's tomorrow night for your birthday, right?" I say.

"I don't really feel like celebrating. I don't feel too well these days."

"Hey honey, I don't think I've said this yet. I feel horrible that your grandfather's sick." I hug her.

"Thanks, Max."

"You could probably stand to think about something else," I say. I feel bad for her — this feeling gives me a new perspective on my troubles. They aren't as great as hers. True. But life would be perfect if only *he* moved out.

She says unconvincingly, "I do need to get out of this house. Maybe it'll give my nerves a rest."

"Great then. We'll take a cab at around seven o'clock."

"Right." Nadia smiles shyly.

I come home from work, have a shower and put on a new navy sports jacket that I've bought for the occasion. I come down the stairs, and because I'm looking forward to an evening alone with my girl I am not even anxious that Chris and Nadia are talking in the kitchen. I let her know that I'm ready to leave; then I sit in the stairwell and wait. Chris talks to Nadia for an interminable length of time, yet I don't have the will to interrupt.

She hurries out of the kitchen. "I have to take a shower."

The sound of running water in the bathroom has a soothing effect on me. Once, in the counsellor's cabin, about twelve of us were making a ruckus, kid's stuff really, playing rugby using a basketball, a pair of bunks acting as end zones, and betting who could huck the ball from the far bunk so that it landed and stayed on the top of the bunk in the connecting cabin. Smiley Wilson came in and told us to cut out the noise because his children were trying to sleep and we were keeping them up. He stood there, with his lips twitching and his eyes bulging, and you were at the sink in the bathroom spraying water into the cabin. Hey Petey, I yelled, stop it! We're keeping Wilson's children up. Only you hadn't known that Smiley was standing there yelling and spitting saliva all over the place. He didn't fire us, though.

Maybe we were lucky, but I think deep down Smiley kinda liked us, no?

That was the night I finally slept with Nadia. I remember taking off her Puma sweats. God, they smelled so lemon fresh. But I wasn't just thinking about sex. I was thinking about you and the guys. I was thinking about what a great time we were having.

Truth is they still talk about us at Skyhawk, Max.

In my brain there are probably just as many bytes of you telling Smiley that his kids are fairies as there are of the first time I had sex with Nadia.

"I'll just be five more minutes, Max," Nadia says.

Chris is suddenly walking down the hall to where I'm standing in the main entrance, but I cut him off. "Could you go back and wait in the living room?"

"What? I just have to get my bag."

I put my hand on his shoulder, and say, "We're never going to get out of here. Just go back to the other room, okay."

"What do you mean?"

"Go away."

Looking embarrassed, Chris says, "Okay. Have a nice time." He retreats and I hear him drop to the sofa.

Nadia emerges from our bedroom wearing eyeliner, nylons and slender knee-high leather boots. She looks into the kitchen and then peers down the hallway that leads to the living room.

"Chris is watching television."

"Oh, right." She picks up her purse and says, "See you later, Chris."

"I'm so sorry I'm in an awful mood, Max," Nadia says. "I'm no fun tonight."

I rub the stubble on my head. "Don't worry about it, honey. It's understandable that you're sad."

With Nadia picking at her asparagus, I drift off. That fucker, Chris, is becoming her confidant. What's more is he's irrevocably stolen my chance to act in this way. I'd love to make her feel better, but she doesn't even want to be here. She can't reconcile that while she's out having dinner with me her grandfather is sick and in danger of dying. What do I do?

"What are you thinking about?"

"This is what I think, honey — I'm going to order some coffee and dessert for us, all right?" I look around the restaurant. A man and woman, formally dressed, are sitting three tables down from us. The guy, about five years older than me, has just bought his date a rose from someone who has wandered into Palermo's from the street. "You see that man and woman," I say quietly. "I know for a fact they aren't getting it on. You want to know how I know? He's been so incredibly, pathetically polite to her. He just bought her a rose. He poured her water, for Christ's sake. You might say that this is nice, right, but I know it isn't getting him anywhere. There's no way he's sleeping with her. If he were, he wouldn't be trying so hard. He wouldn't be talking so much. He's been going on now for three minutes, not making eye contact, barely coming up for air, thinking this is the night, this is the night! But it ain't gonna happen." I fold my arms imperiously. "Just shows you that I am the king at understanding the human animal. That's why you're with me, right, honey?" I say this last bit less assuredly and am glad to hear Nadia giggle, though a half second too late.

"You're definitely gifted, Max," she says. "Can we head home soon?"

She isn't keen to talk. That's okay. During my long recklessly unwarranted appraisal of the other couple's relationship which, now that I think about it, is probably far healthier than ours, a liberating thought popped into my head. Could it be that Chris is out of her league? I mean, look at her. There are blemishes on her cheeks. She's about three inches taller than he is. And she's awkward and far too thin. Maybe I can point this out sometime. Give him a heads up.

I am glad to see that my adversary is in his room. Nadia turns on *Late Night with David Letterman*. We sit on the sofa and I feel good about myself again.

But now he's here with a toothbrush in his mouth, brushing and trying to talk at the same time. His words muffled, he says, "This is not going to do. Letterman is a bit of a sod, don't you think? Now Leno is a real comedian if you ask me. Let's have a go at that, shall we?" He changes the channel to *The Tonight Show with Jay Leno*.

"What makes you think you can just grab the remote and do that?" Nadia says.

Chris affects a British accent, "Oh come on luv. Let's give the lad five minutes. If I can show you in five minutes that Leno is the more talented, well, could we say that you have been converted?"

Nadia, still irritated, says, "Okay. Five minutes."

We watch *The Tonight Show* and Chris highlights the funnier parts of Leno's routine. Nadia makes a sad effort to be contrary.

"If I can get you to agree that Leno is better than Letterman," Chris says, "you have to do my dishes for a week."

"Okay, but after we watch Leno," she says, "we'll watch Letterman for a while and if I can get you to agree that Letterman is better you have to, oh let me see . . . you have to call me 'your majesty' for a week."

"Even in public?"

"Especially in public."

"All right. You've got a bet."

I stand up and say, "You do realize that your bet is inane. Quality is completely subjective. There are no objective measures that you can use to see who has the better show." I look at both of them but don't get any reaction. "If one of you should concede that the other's guy is better, then I am going to puke because it would just be kind of . . . well, stupid."

"I'd agree with you," Chris says. "If it weren't that Leno is so obviously more talented than Letterman. You can see for yourself, Max."

"Oh God!"

"I plan to mess every dish in the house. Make Indian curries with the mixer — and bake lots of desserts this week. We're talking about every dish for one week, right?"

"Every dish," Nadia says.

I am relieved to see that she is looking at me with sadness and concern. I put on my coat, open the door and without saying goodbye, step into the cold night. I walk to Sarah's Pub, where I try to recall the fifteen-minute walk but can't — I haven't been aware of my surroundings. I sit down at the bar, order a pint and when it comes, I drink it quickly. I can think about only one thing: when I left, were they both sitting on the sofa or was one of them on the loveseat? I have a second pint, and try to rewind the events of the night in an effort to mull over Chris's culpability. He *has* flirted with her, but he isn't *trying* to make her like him. His effortlessness, in fact, is what's so infuriating. He's not overtly seducing her, but his personality and looks are enough for this to occur. He's got to have an awareness of this on some level. This is why I despise the fucker, Petey.

You're twice the man he is, Max.

I beckon the bartender. "My girlfriend is at home watching television with one of my buddies from college."

"Maybe you should get back there," he says.

At a table not far from the bar is a group of four guys about my age, who are less sporty and more technology-driven types. They chat about their jobs and people. They rib each other a little but they do so good-naturedly. I feel an affinity to these guys. I even think of asking if I can join them. This is impossible, of course, because I have to think about Nadia and Chris again, and at some point I have to get back there to ensure that they aren't doing it on the sofa. A toxic, lacerating feeling grows in my stomach. I'm normally not the jealous type. I'm actually a very funny person. I'm interesting too. Which isn't to say that I'm funny or interesting or at peace with myself right now. But this isn't me. My thinking right now, my point of view, my *being* has been compromised. Mostly by events out of my control. For this reason the person I thought I was isn't the person I am now. But I'd like to think the person I thought I was *is* who I am. I've been living in these three dimensions: X, Y, and Z. The other Max, the one I thought I was, exists in some other universe with dimensions — say R, S, and T. I'd love to get back to that universe. How do I get there? I know this sounds strange, but I think an awareness of this displacement — this otherness — gets me part way there. I've just got to make it the rest of the way. So far, my plan has been to stay the course. This means leaving the pub, returning to 77 Midland Ave., ignoring that there is a problem, and having faith that this will blow over. That Chris'll move out. Is this how I get back to that other universe? I don't know. Do you follow me, Petey?

Not sure what you're on about, bro'.

The idea of going home makes me feel wretched. Why *do* I have to go back? I could try to travel through some sort of singularity, or I could just move to another place. I laugh out loud and look around to see if anybody thinks I am crazy.

At two o'clock, the bartender asks me to leave. I walk around the neighbourhood for an hour. In the cool air, and in the darkness — the streets are dimly lit on this side street — I decide on a new course of action. A new plan. In my head I compose the note that I will leave for them before I depart for good. I only go back to our house when I've got something witty and yet honest that'll leave them thinking about me for months to come. I go into our room where I quietly pack some of my clothing and belongings in a large suitcase. Nadia's sleeping deeply. At four o'clock in the morning I get a crayon, scarlet-red, and write the note. I tape it on the refrigerator next to some photos of Nadia and me at Camp Skyhawk.

I read the letter out loud.

I know you guys want to sleep together. Why not just go ahead and do it? You have my blessing. Have many children. I don't care. I have a new life or at least I am going to have a new life with new friends that support me. I have released myself from this existence. (And don't tell me you don't know what I am talking about.) I am not bitter at all. Start a family if you want. — Max

Their reaction to this candid assessment of our living arrangement might in fact inhibit them from sleeping together. I giggle. My blessing might restrain them from further flirtation. My note might repel Nadia and cause Chris to become self-conscious. In fact, the very spark of their relationship from day one was lit by my insecurities and, with me gone, who knows? I'm out of here. Am I making a mistake, Petey?

Sometimes a guy needs his freedom, Max.

I put next month's rent in an envelope on the counter. I call a taxi and then quietly lug my suitcase down the driveway. I want to set off quickly before Chris or Nadia wakes up and sees me. Before I leave, I think: What if she doesn't fancy Chris?

It doesn't matter. If she really wants me she can come after me. But what about my furniture: the soiled sofa and loveseat, the television, the dishes and books that have accumulated in our house? I dismiss the thought. I'll be back in the house within a month and all will return to normal, the way things were before Chris moved in with us.

I cross the street to the taxi and get in. From the corner of my eye I see that Chris's light is on in his bedroom and I hear a rattling noise inside the house. The toxic, lacerating feeling returns to my stomach. While the taxi pulls away from the street I wonder: Is she in there? Is she in there with him right now?

AN EMPTY TANK OF GAS

IZZIE AND I SAT IN THE LIVING room, smoking and talking. I was slouching in my reclining chair, my legs resting on a coffee table. Candles glowed near my feet. I got up and gazed out the window at the concrete buildings surrounding our apartment. It was raining, so Izzie was reluctant to take me outside to explore the neighbourhood, Moda. Two weeks ago, Izzie had picked me up at the airport, and brought me back here, though not without incident. In a queue for the *dolmuş*, right next to the Blue Mosque, which looks curiously like the Rogers Centre in Toronto, I got in a shoving match with a young Turk who'd nudged ahead of us in line, my thinking being that no one took advantage of someone from Sarnia, Ontario. Izzie spoke to him in the native tongue and calmed him down until it came time for us to board the *dolmuş*. The shoving match resumed between him and me — with only two seats available, the boy unwisely thought he could snag Izzie's seat.

Seda, a young woman with large brazen eyes, walked, hips swaying, into the living room. Her friends were giggling as they made *mantı*, folding dough around meat, at the kitchen table. The right side of her mouth curled towards her nose and

in a singsong voice she said, "The tank of gas is empty, Izzie."
She stalled on the "z" when she said his name.

Izzie lugged the empty propane tank out the door. Twenty
minutes later he came back dripping wet. The fifty-pound
metal tank banged against his knees. His tiny belly levered
some of the weight and his taut wrists supported the rest. He
set the tank up. Seda brushed the hair out of her eyes, took a
towel and rubbed her Australian boyfriend's head and face.
She joined her friends at the table and after a few seconds
called: "Izzie, could you please get us an ashtray?" The women
all laughed loudly.

I sat down on the sofa from where I could see them. After
Izzie set the ashtray on a placemat, all five feet two inches of
him was pushed from the arms of one woman to the next. The
three women painted his fingernails, painted red circles on his
cheeks and used eyeliner to draw a false moustache so that he
looked like Charlie Chaplin.

"You look like a clown," I said.

Seda pouted. "You don't like Izzie's makeup, Brian?"

I pushed up my lips. "Not really."

"I draw on Izzie means he is mine. Am I right, Izzie?"

"Sure, love." Izzie rolled his eyes. "They're just having fun,
I suppose."

"Why don't you draw on her?" I said.

Seda turned up the Yeni Ufuklar CD five decibels, so that
Izzie and I couldn't have a decent conversation. We got up to
leave. Just as I was going through the doorway Seda smiled.
"Don't worry. We'll find you a Turkish girlfriend, Brian."

What she didn't know was that I had the girl problem
covered. I'd only been here for a few days and I'd already taken
one of the English Fast secretaries for a test drive. Also, the
owner of English Fast, Nazif Bey, had given me the Koç Bank

account, eighteen women in an Intermediate class, all single, all looking at me as if I were the pop singer, Tarkan. I had the pick of the litter, so just the other day, I cornered Gülsev by the second floor washroom, put my hand on hers, lifted her delicate fingers under my tight *Molson Export* T-shirt and got her to feel my chest. The next day in class we were studying the present continuous tense. When it was her turn to think of an example, Gülsev went up to the board and wrote, *Are you having a girlfriend?* I had to ignore this though — didn't want the runners-up to be jealous, right? Blame it on eyes-wide-open exuberance. I was a man who had, before coming here, exclusively dated Wendy, the foul-mouthed, hockey-haired, junior high dropout. I was overwhelmed by the new stimuli. I was in a country whose women were sultry, nicely tarted up, not cynical or suspicious, but sweet. I'd found a system that had proven so far to be foolproof. I got lovely Gülsev to meet me here at the apartment when Izzie and Seda were out, and made it impossible for the dark-skinned, big-eyed bank clerk to turn cold by taking off my shirt, completely inappropriate, but who was going to tell. *İnşallah.* Gülsev must have thought that I was acting typically. She covered up my half-naked body with what was at her disposal, in this case her own, and well . . .

I came home one night, walked into the kitchen. The sink was filled with dishes. Eggplant was splattered on the floor and walls. I wrote a note and placed it on their bedroom door.

Seda,

Don't mean to sound like a nag after you have been so nice to me but cockroaches are going to eat the food off the dishes if we don't clean them.

Brian

In the morning I was drowsing on the sofa when Seda emerged from their room bleary-eyed, wearing silk pyjamas. She said, "Izzie promised to clean."

"Izzie didn't make the mess."

"Don't worry, Brian." She lingered on the "ee" sound in worry. She went back to the bedroom. She came back in a spring dress and said, "Tell him I'll be back in an hour."

After she left, I moved to the patio and watched her flit down the steps and around the corner. I found a bottle of liquid soap under the sink, filled a bucket with water and began scrubbing the caked appliances and the tile on the walls. Izzie came home with bread and cheese. He asked where Seda was. I whipped some suds on the floor and pointed to the door. I said, "She left. Cockroaches are going to get at these dirty plates, Izzie."

"You're absolutely right, Brian," Izzie said. "I'll have a word with her when she gets back."

She didn't come back that night or the next. Izzie, in his grey sweatpants, curled up with a magazine on the sofa. His eyes were fixed on the table in front of him.

He lay there for two days except for intermittent smoke breaks on the balcony. When she came back, he sprang to his feet. "Come in here," he said, in a way that made me want to cheer. She went into their bedroom.

"Give her a healthy tongue lashing," I said. Head down, he entered their room. I'm sad to say that the only tongue-lashing I heard through our thin walls was from Seda.

The next evening Izzie and I smoked cigarettes on the balcony. Three storeys below a man pulled a wagon and chanted. He dropped the cart and collected some pans from a veiled elderly lady.

"What did you do when you were in Australia?" I said.

"I was a chef at a number of lower-end restaurants," Izzie said. "The work was all right but I didn't like the hours. I lived with a woman for ten years. I didn't fancy her much, so I quit my job, broke off with her and got a charter flight to Turkey."

Izzie smiled at me, stubbed out his cigarette and said, "This place is all right. You'll get used to the people. They're just like us — they work, and relax on the weekend just like us." He breathed an excessive amount of air through his nose and said, "Even the smell in the air — the diesel from the buses mixed with the mosquito insecticide. You'll get used to it. That smell makes me giddy."

One sunny morning I followed Izzie outside to explore a part of the city. The little Australian bounced up the narrow streets of Taksim. He ignored the aggressive young males. We dropped into mosques and teahouses. At the market, he spewed Turkish at the busy owner. He came away with armfuls of bread, fruit and vegetables. He was charming with the people in the market and confident with the language. Only on the odd occasion would he search his mind for the exact word that he wanted to use. A Turk with a moustache stepped in front of us and said in broken English, "Do you want some of this jewelry?"

The large Turk laughed at Izzie's response. After we'd walked away I asked him what he'd said.

"I told him we're just poor English teachers and that we don't have any money."

We wriggled through the crowd in tandem. His cowboy boots didn't slow him down. His tight pants gripped his thin legs and when he ran or shifted gears he couldn't bend his knees properly. He looked like a diminutive doll as he squeezed between heavy Turkish women, jumped over pots and pans and avoided pushy vendors. From time to time I lost sight of him. He led me through a myriad of narrow cobblestone streets and, with one eye on the terrain, fed me a wealth of information: Atatürk; the histories of various mosques and the meaning of "call to prayer"; the indignities perpetrated by the local police; the little drummer boy in the month of *Ramazan*; the joy of invitations for dinner from genuinely curious students; the locations of remote candle-lit pubs. He introduced me to *iskender kebab, mantı, ayran* and the generosity of the people, the beauty of the women and the hot-headed nature of the males. That night I lay in my room, thoughts of Istanbul in my head, everywhere the dark-skinned, dark-eyed beauties contrasting with my paleness. Like Izzie had said, the North American birds just couldn't compete here. I agreed wholeheartedly, their faces spinning in my brain until I finally fell asleep.

A few days later Seda brought home her cousin, a stocky young man. Izzie got up, went to the kitchen, chopped some apples and then served them to their guest, who wore a Rage Against the Machine T-shirt and, aside from the initial greeting, had had nothing to say to Izzie or me. He observed us disdainfully for a while, and then got up from the sofa and wandered through the apartment.

Seda, Izzie and I shared a cigarette on the balcony. Heat from the living room escaped into the cool night air. I took a puff from the cigarette, passed it to Seda and said, "You and your cousin — are you guys close?"

Seda looked at me. "What do you mean? He's my cousin."

"Right."

Fifteen minutes later Seda grabbed her cousin's arm and they left. That night Seda came home at six o'clock in the morning. *"Başka erkek arkadaşın mı var?"* Izzie asked.

"Leave me alone," Seda said. She showered and then left again for another eighteen hours.

Over the next two weeks Izzie wore the same gray pants day after day. His hair was unkempt. Particles of fluff stuck to the grease that plastered the side of his head. He arrived to class just minutes before the bell. His writing on the board was sloppy and one morning he was reproached at break by a colleague for misspelling the word 'where'. Izzie had written 'whore.'

My own class was in turmoil because, in the middle of a fascinating lesson on the past perfect tense, Jülide, a sprightly checkout girl at the Koç Bank, completely unaware of my attachment to Gülsev, chose this sentence, grammatically spot on, to write on the whiteboard: *Brian had already taken off his shirt before I walked into his apartment.* She highlighted the past perfect construction, '*had already taken*' in red marker, to contrast with the standard black. She, of course, found this funny (evidently, "Let's have some discretion about this, honey" didn't translate well into Turkish), as did sixteen of the other nubile bank clerks, but unfortunately Gülsev, the eighteenth, took exception, precipitating a battle in Turkish between the two women, all verbs at the beginning of sentences, nouns with suffixes. Though I'd mastered the twenty most-used words in the language, I didn't understand what was being said, so I was completely caught off guard when Gülsev maneuvered around the desks to the front where I stood. It was there that *she* unpredictably took off *her* shirt, and flicked it at me. Her bra was twisted, pushing one of her boobs in a downward direction. She walked out without her blouse — just a little dramatic, I thought, but I also wondered why I was so turned on.

℃

On a Friday morning I woke up and heard Seda outside my door. "Izzie's things are missing," she said. "Where is Izzie? Did he tell you where he was going, Brian?"

"No. Is he not here?" I got up and looked into their room. Izzie's clothing and belongings were all gone. I went back to my mattress and tried to rest for another hour. Finally, I gave up and put the kettle on the stove. Seda sat on the sofa with her head between her hands. She cried softly. "Where is he? Where could Izzie go?" Her shoulders gently shook. When she said his name, saliva sprayed from her lips. I tried to console her but she didn't listen. Eventually she got up and left. She came back a couple of days later while I was at work and collected her things.

Some teachers from school and I sat around a small round table in a pub in the centre of Kadıköy, a plate of *dolma* between us. I'd found one of Izzie's sweaters and was passing it around to teachers, who marvelled at how cute it was. With a hammer and some nails borrowed from the bartender, I nailed the sweater on the wall. Each teacher in turn then bowed in mock reverence to it. There were rumours of his whereabouts: he'd turned female impersonator, working for an old-school theatre company that only employed men, giving him access to the best parts. He was in Izmir, studying to become a chess grandmaster. He was in a stall in the bathroom, biding his time, waiting to spring out at the first ex-pat that he recognized.

A few weeks later Seda returned to our flat in Moda. She had sunburned cheeks, a musty fishy smell and her hair stuck damply to the back of her head. She looked like a lost kitten. Had she been running through the Istanbul sewage tunnels? She sat on the sofa and I got her a cup of tea. She said, "Do you mind if I stay here for one night? I'll get out of your hair tomorrow. I promise."

I put two cups of tea on the night table and sat next to her. Off came my shirt — always a sure thing, though eight months of nightly *pide* had taken its toll. My paunch was distended over my belt and wobbled when I moved. (The *pide* stales over night, so you must finish it completely in one sitting.) I leaned across her body and held her left elbow. There was a fearful look in her eyes. She shuffled back on her elbows and like a mangy street cat inched towards the end of the sofa. I backed off and without turning to look at her I hastily retreated to my bedroom. I woke up at five-thirty in the morning. The shower was running. By six o'clock she was gone.

Over the next month I made new friends. From time to time talk of Izzie and Seda surfaced but for the most part I'd forgotten about them. A new teacher had failed to report and so Izzie and Seda's old room remained empty. I ventured to the Blue Mosque again, this time by myself. On the ferry ride across the Bosphorus — misting, seagulls swarming the polluted seawater — I bought a miniature-sized cup of tea from a young vendor and was mesmerized by her raw sex appeal. I offered to help her with her business, and tried to sell the cups of tea to other Turks, who ignored me. In case you are wondering, I *did* take off my shirt, not to seduce the dark-haired vendor, but rather to soak up some rays. None of the other males on the ship stripped themselves of even their dark suit jackets. I never made it to the Blue Mosque, which is a pity because from a distance it looked impressive in the setting sun. I spent the return trip trying to find the vendor and, arriving back in Kadıköy, I gave up on all cultural sites.

In September I came home one day and heard a noise in the kitchen. I stopped in the hallway. A head of long black hair bobbed in the doorway of the kitchen. I said, "Who's there?" It was Seda. She disappeared into the kitchen, then re-emerged with a small person pinned between her white T-shirt and her chest. She had pulled her shirt over his head and torso. Tufts of black hair curled over the collar of her shirt and his nose looked as if it might penetrate the cloth. With a flurry, she pulled back her shirt and I got a brief glimpse of her brassiere.

I clapped the little Australian on the back.

"Couldn't be away from my girl for long," Izzie said. "Don't mind if we move back in, do you?"

That evening Seda cooked dinner. Jülide was over. We were playing our favourite game, the one where she mounted my knee — always her initiative, God bless her — and I jauntily bounced her up and down like she was a professional jockey. I whinnied in her ear and she gripped my pants so tightly I thought they might tear at the seam. Seda came into the living room and looked at us disapprovingly. "I've got two knees, Seda." I said.

"We need gas," she said.

Izzie gave me a wary glance and got up from his seat.

Seda motioned for Izzie to sit down and said, "You don't need to go, Izzie." She gave me a penetrating look.

I got up from the sofa, unable to look at Izzie. I got the empty tank of gas, hoisted it to my hip and descended the stairs.

THE RUNNER

CAROL AND I ARE COMING UP THE stairs at the Eglinton subway entrance. A sweater is tucked under my arm. People are cheering and whistling. Horns are sounding. I grab Carol's hand and guide her to an area on the sidewalk where we can see the race. A young, thin Kenyan marathoner is running effortlessly down Yonge Street. This gives the event an immediate, authentic feel. Like when I was up north camping and saw an owl. Another Kenyan, taller and with a high forehead, is behind him. These two are way ahead of all the other marathoners. A middle-aged man, short and pudgy is jogging by with a woman in her late twenties. She's got a thin upper body and is congenitally heavy from the waist down. They're obviously in a different event.

The weather is sunny and it's a few degrees above zero on this October morning. At the corner of Yonge and Eglinton, the seven-km mark, Carol and I wait near Chapters for Jeremy, Ross and Wendy — all from my office at INCO — to come down the hill. They're in the 10 km race. I observe the runners with reverence, thankful that I'm watching from the sidewalk. The last thing I'd ever want to do on a Sunday morning is run. It's still early, and the pack of front-runners is tight. I don't expect to see our friends for a while. Two speakers the size of closets boom in the background. Mad Dog and Billie, local DJs from Mix FM, are in front of Starbucks. Mad Dog yells into the microphone, "Go 103! Go 103!" Number 103 tilts his head toward the ground as if he doesn't want the attention.

I was in Chapters last Monday at the Health and Medicine area. It was pleasantly empty of people and the chest-level shelves meant that I could see anyone coming toward me. The *Oxford Encyclopedia of Medicine*, page 276, had unpleasant images of electrolysis, skin grafts, pink flaps of skin, and discussed the removal of unwanted hair follicles. After three hours, I put the book back on the shelf. My leg was asleep, so I stretched it. I was walking to my car when I thought, "Wait a second," and turned around and headed back up the escalator to look up the cost of the procedure. It was reasonable, about a month's salary. This could happen.

The second tier of marathoners is going by — a mix of Africans and Mexicans, all slightly built, and running easily. I'm surprised to see Randy with them. He's struggling like a wounded antelope trying to keep up with the herd, scanning the crowd like a small child at the zoo, turning his head in all directions. Has someone called his name? He's wearing a Dri FIT pullover top and Clima-FIT overlay and Air Pegasus shoes. In front of Starbucks, he slows to take a small cup of water from a volunteer.

He pitches the cup on the street and stumbles, quickly regaining his balance. He runs another block until he's reached Berwick Avenue. Beyond this point the crowd thins. Two blocks further there's no one watching or cheering. On this lonely stretch two marathoners pass him and he steps off Yonge Street onto the sidewalk. "Why has Randy stopped running?" I ask Carol.

"I've no idea," she says. "It's strange."

We watch him walk the sidewalk parallel to the runners, but in the opposite direction. He walks by Hansa Language School, past Canada Square and The Mandarin Restaurant, through the Yonge-Eglinton intersection, past Mad Dog and Billie and the Mix FM crew. He's pulling a tank top over his number, concealing it. He's behind the crowd now, walking near Carol and me. "Hey Randy," I say, but he doesn't hear me. He's strolling aimlessly, but he's careful not to get too close to the street. He keeps going up the hill, past Pizza Pizza, past a sushi restaurant.

The sun is shining, which makes me feel good. I lean against Carol, breathing on her neck, but then I'm aware that my breath might smell, so I bury my nose in her scarf and hug her tightly. "Do you want some pizza, honey?" I say. "I can get us some pizza."

"No thanks, Alan," she says. "I might get something a little later. It's only eleven o'clock."

"Right. Later," I say. "Tell you what — you should run in one of these next year."

"Yeah, right."

"No really. You're a great little athlete. I've seen you play volleyball. You're great. I could be your coach. We'll start training tomorrow."

"I don't think it's really my thing," she says softly.

"I think you'd be great at it."

I remember a recent morning, Wednesday or Thursday, around seven o'clock. I was in bed, not wanting to get up. Carol put on a Dido CD then came into my room — our room — with a bowl of corn flakes in her wholesome hands, sugar dusted on the cereal, and a tiny cup of orange juice nestled between her elbow and ribs. She was trying to conceal her cheery, no-need-to-thank-me look. I said, "Oh, thanks, honey. It's time for me to get up for work."

She sat on the side of our bed in her blue flannel pyjamas, near a Nike print of a black Labrador wearing running shoes. "I think Dido has to be my favourite band. If I could only take one CD to a deserted island it would be Dido."

"How can it be your favourite?" I said. "I just bought you that CD two weeks ago."

"Still, I love her music."

"But how can you say it's your favourite when you've only heard her for two weeks?"

"Yeah, but I'd heard her music before."

"When I put it on you even asked me who it was."

"But I'd heard it before," she says plaintively. "I just wasn't sure when you first put it on, but I've definitely heard it before." She was quietly staring at the bed. She probably should have taken back the corn flakes. Especially since she'd been so sweet, and I'd been so rude. I could only think of one thing — not Dido's music, not that she'd just made me breakfast (albeit a rather rudimentary one). I was thinking about the black wisps of hair on her upper lip.

A loud horn goes off. People are cheering loudly. A spectator on the street gives number 345, probably his wife or girlfriend, a small cup of Gatorade, and takes her picture. Another runner has to take a wide berth to avoid bumping into him.

"I think Randy dropped out of the race," I say.

"I know," Carol says. "I wonder why he stopped running. He didn't look tired. That's bizarre."

"When you're in it next year you won't stop, will you honey?"

I sometimes feel that when Carol and I are in public, we're just friends. That there is something fundamental, like a lack of passion, that differentiates our relationship from other common-law and marital relationships I've observed. For example, there's a man and a woman standing by a mailbox, balloons in their hands, sharing an ice-cream cone. I'd never share ice-cream with Carol. She'd get her saliva on the nuts. She's not the most delicate eater. Maybe I should share an ice-cream cone with her in public, just to prove something, but I'd likely be repulsed during the entire ice-cream-cone-sharing experience, so what would be the point?

Ice cream? I was eating ice cream and pie just last Thursday at Swiss Chalet. I recognized Randy's voice coming from a booth in front of ours. He was facing a quixotic couple. From the tone of their voices and by the way they gingerly nursed their coffees, it was obvious that they weren't there for dinner. The lady was saying, "I think young people today are very confused. It's not always easy for you guys. You've got it tough."

"I come to this place just to feel noticed," Randy said. "Sometimes I come here just to have someone recognize me and treat me nicely. The waitress actually smiles at me. Becky is super friendly. Then, one day I saw her being nice to this old guy — not that I begrudged him. It's just that I realized that I was looking for something a little more than to be treated well in a restaurant."

I'd never say something that would leave me that vulnerable. This was manipulation — he was saying this so they'd pity him. I'd never want someone to pity me. I wonder, though, if the older man quietly despised Randy. From where

I was sitting I couldn't read his face. The lady touched Randy's hand and told him that he'd done the right thing by calling them for help. The Lord would get him through this. Anytime Randy needed to talk he could call. She told him to take up something of interest — cooking, playing a sport, or maybe joining a church group.

"You have to let me pay for your coffee," Randy said. "You people are so nice and I want to show my appreciation. I know you guys are just doing a bit of charity work today, but I really appreciate you spending the time."

"We're not doing charity work," the lady said. "You're a fine young person. You just need to find something in life that makes you happy — something that you find interesting."

"I've got an idea," Randy says. "Some of my colleagues at work are running in a race this weekend. Maybe I can join them."

I've been at this stultifying race for thirty minutes now. After the Kenyans, everyone else seems like an amateur. I cheer for a young lad with a headband as he runs by. The kid is earnest, just like every other runner. Our friends should be jogging by soon, but that doesn't excite me. The only interesting part of the morning so far has been Randy. Why isn't he in the race anymore? He took a left at the Bank of Montreal, on Orchard View Street. The sun has faded behind some clouds and it's getting chilly. I offer Carol my sweater. When she declines, I put it on. I tell her I want to see what Randy's up to. I walk up the hill toward Pizza Pizza. My eyes are on the sidewalk ahead. There he is, just ten yards in front of me, at the Hero's sandwich shop, trying to get back to the street. He taps someone on the shoulder. "Excuse me," he says. "I need to get back in the race." He edges his way between two large ladies and walks onto Yonge Street, almost knocking into an older marathoner. He's stretching his calf muscles. I yell out his name. This time he turns his head and makes eye contact.

Two nights ago, Carol came home late from work. I was lying on the black leather sofa watching my third consecutive episode of *Everybody Loves Raymond*. I'd called in sick because, when I woke up at 7:00, I felt a tickle at the back of my throat.

"You could have cleaned up around here," she said.

Play Station discs were on the carpet. Apple peels and spilt berries from the smoothie I'd made were still on the kitchen counter. IAMS cat food was all over the floor because I'd accidentally tripped and knocked the bowl with my foot. "I'll get to it in a second," I said.

"What are we going to have for dinner?" she said.

I looked at her. She was wearing a black business suit and her hair was tied in a bun. Her nylons had a run and her makeup was partly smudged. "We can order in," I said. "I'm still not feeling too shit hot."

She went to the bedroom and shut the door. I felt guilty, but only for a while. I didn't want to stare at it anymore, the moustache, that is, and with her in the bedroom I could do some more thinking about my options.

When I get back to my spot beside Carol in front of Silver City and Chapters, she nudges me. "Here they are," she says.

Jeremy, Ross, and Wendy are running so slowly that they could be walking. Wendy, in particular, looks out of place.

Normally she's in a business suit. Today, she's wearing blue shorts and a T-shirt. Her face is red. Given the chilly weather she's not really appropriately dressed. When she sees us she smiles sheepishly, as if she's embarrassed. She looks silly, but she's bravely willing herself forward. Jeremy and Ross are flanking her, like they do at work.

Carol yells, "You look great! Keep it up."

Wendy, Ross, and Jeremy have passed us before I yell, "Great job, guys!" I hope they heard me.

Carol and I walk back to the subway station. We're taking it to Davisville, so as to be in position to cheer for them at the end of their race. I look at Yonge Street one more time. Randy is running down this section again, although this time with an ungainly limp.

"Here he comes," I say. "Look, Randy's coming this way again."

He picks up speed as he passes Mad Dog and Billie for the second time. Mad Dog says, "This guy is really trucking!" Randy hears this and does a jig, clicks his heels together in the air. He almost falls. He passes other runners and, like when he ran down this part of the street earlier, he's looking furiously at the crowd. A group of young ladies cheer for him. He slows down and comes to a full halt in order to talk with them. The three girls look squeamish. After an uncomfortable-looking exchange of greetings, Randy has a difficult time starting again. He doesn't go far. I'm not astonished to see that once again he takes a right turn off the course and onto Berwick Avenue.

Again I follow him. He lowers himself to the grass beside the Hansa Language School parking lot, where he takes off his shoes and socks. Big blisters are swelling on his feet. "Next year you'll finish the thing, Randy!" I say.

"Hey, Alan. I thought I saw you," he says. He gets up and hobbles barefoot over to the side of the curb and looks at the runners passing by. I think he's pondering the possibility that he might have been able to finish. I want to tell him that it's not the attention from the crowd that's rewarding but the training, the striving, the self-improvement and the actual running itself. If he were to genuinely try, his enthusiasm would make him attractive to others, which would take care of his primary needs, friendship and love, but a fleeting thought fills me with despair, the thought that I am he, that he is I.

Yesterday evening my thoughts started to be more obsessive — I wanted to broach the subject, but didn't because I'd hurt Carol's feelings. I went back and forth in my head, rehearsing the conversation. She had no idea what was going on, but she could sense my anxiety. I grabbed her and kissed her on the lips to prove to myself that it was no big deal. I'd shaved assiduously that evening so as not to confuse my bristles with hers. I held her face, venturing my upper lip on hers, at first certain that I indeed did detect the wispy hairs, but when I pulled away I was less sure and wanted to kiss her again, but she pulled back. I wondered if she were tiring of me, but just for a second, because her moustache once again infiltrated my thoughts.

The afternoon has been building up to this moment. Randy's sitting on the grass, putting on clean socks. We're alone. I want to seize the moment and I don't care how I sound. "Hey Randy, how would you feel if your girlfriend — well, let's suppose you had a girlfriend — if she had facial hair? How would you feel about that?" When Randy doesn't immediately say anything, I say, "Hair, right here," I point to my own upper lip.

"Bit of a moustache," he says. He laughs. I also laugh. I'm relieved because he understands, but, just as I'm feeling better, he says, "That sort of thing doesn't bug me." And he tells me about his plans to go to the Dominican Republic in January. I'm nodding, giving him feedback to show I'm listening. I'm pretty sure he's a decent guy. If he knew how much I've been suffering, he'd probably want to help me.

I need to think about something else. I haven't been sleeping much. I've been obsessively ruminating about Carol's moustache for six days straight. This can't be good. I try to think about something else — the Maple Leafs, the three goslings in the stream near our apartment, my lovely arthritis-plagued mother, Carol's gorgeous legs. I try to replace the image of her moustache with the image of her pretty legs, but this is a mistake because I end up with a hybrid image, which sullies the legs. I think about how she's always straightening my glasses. This is tender. I try to muster the warm feeling that came over me when she last straightened them, maybe some tears, but I get nothing. None of these other thoughts are compelling.

There must be something that I haven't figured out yet. I review the facts: One, I'm not vain. Two, I want to marry her, although I do acknowledge that this is just to prove that I'm not vain. Three, Randy isn't bothered by facial hair on a girl. Four, when I kissed her I was unsure whether I felt anything or not. Five, she has great legs. Six, she could always get electrolysis, and in my closet under some sheets is a pamphlet from Dr. Granger's institute, with phone numbers and a website. All of these thoughts take one minute thirty-four seconds.

I turn away so that Randy can't see that I'm an agitated mess. I want to get away from here. Carol must be waiting. Randy is smiling, and this makes me feel even worse — that it is Randy who has normal feelings, and who can see what truly matters, while I'm the one with the unhealthy fixation.

A Wonderful Holiday

Russell lay in bed, still wearing his light-blue pyjamas. He was watching *Magnum P.I.* T.C.'s helicopter had a bullet hole and Magnum was explaining to T.C. that he'd compensate him for the damage.

A solitary model airplane, a Sopwith Camel, hung from the ceiling of his room. This was a vestige of his childhood. He had cleared out all the other silly remnants two years before. The Sopwith Camel had been in such pristine condition that he couldn't take it down. Were he to get a girlfriend — this winter, he hoped — he'd be sure to trash it. With his computer and printer, television and stereo system set up along the north wall, and with a proper queen-sized bed, and with beige paint covering the old wallpaper (which had been spotted with lizards), his life now was almost complete. He just had to find a girl. He would move all of his belongings into a two-bedroom condominium when they got married. He'd be nicer to Mom then. He'd even do the dishes here more often if he *weren't* living at home, though on second thought, he'd probably have enough chores of his own to do. The trip he felt obliged to go on was getting in the way of all of his plans. He'd thought of nothing else for a while now.

His mother appeared in the doorway. Her skin was turning a dull grey and her blonde hair was thinning. "I made a nice lunch for you, Russ. Some leftover stew from last night and a piece of the peach cake. You can eat while you wait for your plane."

"Thanks, Ma."

"Have you packed yet?"

He stared at the television, at Magnum, who was yelling at Higgins. It was Sunday. Ray was probably snug in bed, watching the same episode. Just four months ago, Ray and he had graduated from U of T — engineering. They both had entry-level surveyor jobs at different firms. Ray's parents had given him a used Honda Accord as a graduation gift. Russell's mother had made him ask for a week off in the autumn as a condition of his acceptance of this job.

"Russell, have you packed?"

"I'm getting there, ma," he said quietly. He felt like he was ten years old — like his mother was prodding him to get ready for a bantam league baseball practice. He flipped his covers off, climbed out of bed, and put his black suitcase onto the leather sofa-chair.

"I called your boss today, Russell. I reminded him that you won't be back from Vietnam until Tuesday the 27th and not on the Monday like you'd told him. There's no reason you couldn't have told him this yourself yesterday. You're not giving him the best impression, Russ."

"I know, Ma. I know." The only good thing about this trip was that he wouldn't have to work. Only four months into his job and he was already uninspired. Work till seven. His mother's crap cooking at seven-thirty, and at eight, his one pleasure in life — battling it out with Ray as to who could build the greatest empire. Was there Internet access in Saigon? He took off his pyjamas and stood in his boxer shorts scrounging around for a pair of jeans that were hidden under a pile of magazines and laundry. He dug up the jeans, wriggled them on and said, "I'm not a kid, ma."

"You don't look as if you've packed enough clothes. Did you pack a raincoat? It's supposed to rain a lot."

"No. Do you have one that I can borrow?"

She left the room and returned with a raincoat. She opened his suitcase, rearranged some of its contents, placed the folded coat on top and then zipped it up. She handed him a Ziploc bag full of tiny Canadian pins. "I got these at the tourist shop at Harbourfront yesterday. Maybe you can give these to all the nice people that you're going to meet." She was smiling in a way that irritated him.

"Sounds like the taxi is here, Ma."

She was now holding back tears, her eyes and mouth quivering, which had the odd effect of making her look furious. Even though he looked different from his parents, he knew they loved him as much as they loved his older sister. He was suddenly feeling intense sadness, like he might cry as well. They walked down the hallway together. He dragged the suitcase along the hardwood floor. She gave him a beseeching stare. "Pick it up. You're going to leave a scratch. And I don't want to scold you just before you leave." She pecked him on the cheek and quickly shooed him into the taxicab.

Russell didn't dare look at his mother as the cab pulled away. On the plane he forced himself to disregard the source of his queasiness — the fact that he hadn't called his boss to remind him about the change in his travel plans. He also brooded about how he was going to pass an entire week in Vietnam.

℮

After getting off the plane he was preoccupied with two tasks. The first he accomplished in the washroom of the Tan Son Nhat International Airport. He stood in a stall with pants down and both feet on either side of a hole. Worried that someone might interrupt him, he locked the door and jutted his backside against it. He looked down the vast hole and winced. He couldn't see anything but dark. He folded the cuffs of his pants so that they didn't make contact with the slimy tile surface. *Why is this place so gross?* he thought. He listened to men shuffling to urinals, clearing throats and washing their hands, as he crouched down, pinned his belt with his elbow, and strapped his passport to his left leg with duct tape. He used enough tape to entirely hide the document.

The second task required a taxi.

"You are here for women?" the cab driver said. He had the thickest neck Russell had ever seen. "You know, sexy-sexy."

"How much is this ride going to cost?" Russell said.

"Seven dollar," the cabbie said, holding up seven fingers, the car veering slightly into the right lane. "I have three girlfriends. You know, fuck-fuck. Do you have girlfriend?" He laughed and a thin line of red betel nut juice dribbled down his chin.

"No, I don't. Look, I don't mean to be rude but I have to do something important right now."

"No problem," the cab driver said, tapping his steering wheel.

Russell took out his stash of U.S. one-dollar bills. He set aside seven for the driver, then created two piles. The big pile he placed into his wallet. He then bent down and stuffed twenty bills into his sock. If something were to happen in the city — a knife in his ribs, a starving flock of hungry peasants — he was prepared to relinquish his wallet. He'd give it up to the first person who demanded him to do so. He knew he could recover the hidden money from his sock, which he could use for cab fare to the airport. He was confident that, if necessary, he could live off the remaining thirteen dollars, eating noodles and drinking restroom water for a few days while hanging out at the airport and waiting for his plane to take off.

The clerk at the Norfolk Hotel was a middle-aged woman. "*Toi co the giup gi duoc anh,*" she said. Russell told her that he didn't understand, and laughed in embarrassment.

"My name is Huong." She stuck out her tiny hand.

"Hi, I'm Russell."

"You are handsome boy."

He blushed.

"Let me get your key, sweetie." He'd thought that only North Americans could affect this type of familiarity with strangers. The disinfected ambience of the Norfolk lobby felt comfortable. He wished that he could drop his luggage on the linoleum floor, pull up his jeans, saunter over to the leather sofa, and spend time with Huong. She was smiling warmly from the other side of the marble registry desk, holding out his key.

"Do you think I can use your computer to email my parents?" he asked.

"Sure, but it'll cost you five thousand American dollars."

Flustered, he tried to think of something, of some way to correct her, but then she exposed two rows of teeth, like Chiclets. Her tiny hand on his soothed him. "Just joking, sweetie. Of course you can."

The window of his dingy room offered a sweeping view. In front of the open kitchens men sat on stools, almost squatting. They smoked and played dominoes in groups. Russell watched the hustle of the city. A bare-chested man pulled up in a small van, got out and delivered a dozen jugs of water to the hotel. Women carried bags of carrots and cabbage from the market. Children played soccer in an alley. Bicycles and cars bucked frenetically against the grain. Traffic flowed centrifugally around the roundabout in four directions. Motorized rickshaw drivers rode up and down the strip, looking for tourists.

Seeing four soldiers in their dull green fatigues drinking tea at an outdoor cafe reassured him that he was correct in playing it safe. Staying inside his hotel room, he felt protected from mayhem and also from the threat of service. He'd read in his *Lonely Planet* that all young males were required to serve two years in the Vietnam People's army. He imagined that, upon leaving his hotel, he'd be surrounded by soldiers, questioned as to how he'd evaded service and then escorted to a base, where he'd be forced to do calisthenics.

Russell got down on the floor, covered his legs with the stale blanket and thumbed the remote control. After five hours of this — the blanket wrapped around both legs — his left hamstring cramped. He rolled over. His cheek rested on the thin, soiled carpet. Dust particles made him sneeze. He wiped the mucus on his hand into the carpet. As he pulled himself to his knees by grabbing the leg of the bed, he glimpsed a dust-coated magazine nestled under the box spring. He crawled on his knees to the bar fridge, which glistened white against the dull, greyish colours of the carpets, wallpaper and the bedspread, and took out the last of the Kit Kats. He licked the chocolate off the wafer centre and stared at Sean Thompson, the CNN analyst quoting prices on the Hong Kong stock exchange. How had the television screen remained dry and dust-free in this humidity? It dripped from the walls, from the bathroom mirror and from the ceiling. He unstuck himself from the blanket, stood up and explored each cavity of the room, the empty drawers beside the bed, the closet (stocked with towels) and all bathroom receptacles (empty, aside from a toothpaste-coated comb stuck to the back of a middle drawer). He wondered what Ray was doing right now. It'd be what? Ten AM in Toronto?

He decided to go downstairs.

Huong was speaking on the phone, her back slightly turned. The language was alien to him. He found Vietnamese neither pleasing nor displeasing to the ear. Her voice droned on while he curled on the sofa, observing businessmen of various nationalities walk from the elevator to the lobby exit. Waves of humid air reached him from outside. It soaked into the lobby and then receded quickly, the air-conditioned cool reclaiming lost territory.

"Where are you from, sweetie?" Huong was smiling at him. She was wearing an *ao dai*, a long tunic with loose fitting pants.

"Canada — Toronto to be exact." He said this self-consciously, not entirely trusting his voice. His vocal cords had been inactive for three days and so they needed to warm up before he could talk.

"Were you born there?"

He was used to people asking him this. He usually answered in rote manner, but with Huong he found himself searching for an interesting way to tell her at least part of his life story.

Five Australian tourists came into the lobby. Their chubbiness and ruddy faces jarred him into realizing just how extraordinarily skinny the Vietnamese were. He was undersized himself, but aside from the cab driver on the ride in, a freakish anomaly, Russell was about twenty pounds heavier than the Vietnamese men.

When Huong addressed the Aussies, she smiled with an intensity of warmth and good humour that — even though he understood otherwise — he'd hoped she'd reserved only for him. A little depressed, he returned to his room, and for the first time in three days his containment needled him, and the musty smell, mixed with his own odour, repulsed him.

The next morning, he lay in bed until ten o'clock, when hunger pangs got him up. The hotel's nice breakfast, coffee with bread and jam, was not enough. He'd emptied the bar fridge of its chocolate bars and assorted nuts on each of the three days he'd spent in the room. He felt the sort of wooziness one feels after forgoing nourishing food for an extended period of time. And so, like a bed-ridden invalid recovering from an illness and venturing outside for the first time, Russell, with passport firmly strapped to the inside of his leg and his money belt secure, waved goodbye to Huong and took his first weary steps into the polluted streets of Saigon. His first impression was that he could smell the heat in the air — a fruity smell, mixed with garbage.

The food merchants, located on every corner, were all similar — women cleaning pots and pans over sewers. The smell of fish sauce everywhere. Large vats of bubbling broth were exposed to the dirty air and buzzing flies. The patios, some full of foreigners, extended out to the street and were equipped with clean tablecloths and plastic chairs. Russell looked till he found a merchant of about his age.

She had delicate features, a thin nose and perfectly symmetrical eyes, with teeth that were less than white. He stared at her while she chopped some Serrano peppers. Her skin was like tofu. A limp noodle hung precipitously on her white shirt between her petite breasts. He fought off the urge to tap it into the wok that she wiggled with her narrow hips.

Did she watch TV at night? Did she think he was handsome? Did she even have these types of feelings? The Vietnamese people seemed like automatons, like the tiny, inanimate figures in *Age of Empires.*

She asked him something in Vietnamese.

"Pardon me?"

"You speak English?"

"Yes, heh-heh. Only English. Sorry." He hunched his shoulders and held up his hands, palms open to the sky, to show he was inadequate at her language, though he was sure that some atavistic mechanism in his brain was kicking in, which would enable him to understand some Vietnamese by the end of his trip.

He pointed to the rice noodles and asked for chicken. He held out a row of five one-dollar bills. The woman pouted churlishly, took one of the bills and said, "Sit there please." He obeyed. He stared at a small television that was positioned on a crate on the other side of the steel kitchen. Detective Sipowitz was banging a guy's head into a subway door. Russell couldn't hear anything because the set was muted.

"You get *NYPD Blue* on television," he said, pointing at the set.

"Eat your noodles," she said.

Russell studied her over the next two days — the arguments that she had with her husband, the routine of her duties and the efficient way she moved in a contained area. When he'd first met her, he'd doubted her sentience. Her beauty had been abstract. He felt as if he were fawning over a porcelain doll. The more he talked with her the more he saw that she, too, liked to chitchat and laugh with friends, and that she, too, got tired and grumpy in the heat. The fact that she had a cell phone was hilarious. He also felt an ugly jealousy toward her husband, especially when he found out that they had two small babies, who were being looked after by an elderly grandparent.

On the sixth day, Russell learned her name — Thanh Ha. He was chewing on squid, something he'd never tried before. He removed a grey, half-eaten chunk from his mouth, wrapped it in a handkerchief and put it in the breast pocket of his shirt.

"Give it to me," she said. He took the squid-stuffed handkerchief and handed it to her. She put this in the pocket of her apron. A sign of familiarity? *I obviously don't repulse her.* With her this close Russell tried to smell her, but, with the chili sauce from his fried squid still in the air and the sudsy stream of dishwashing water running under his stool, he couldn't detect her scent. Her calves poked from a slit in her tunic. Thicker than he'd supposed for such a delicate woman. He stood up and stretched lazily. "Hey, Thanh Ha. I have to get going." He displayed the American one-dollar bills — was it presumptuous of him to assume that all meals cost a dollar? He smiled, and indicated with a finger the similarities that existed between him and Thanh Ha: the black hair, the dirty T-shirt and the same approximate height. He said, "The same. The same. All the same."

Thanh Ha frowned and shook her head. She pointed to the row of bills in Russell's hand. "Not the same. You eat here. You sleep at the Norfolk Hotel. I today live on four dollars. Tomorrow four dollars. Tomorrow, tomorrow four dollars." She added, "You can go. We want get ready for dinner."

On the day before he left, Russell put on a T-shirt that advertised WJOC Rock, a pair of slacks, and sandals. After taking out four dollars, he placed the wallet inside his suitcase. He went downstairs at seven o'clock, just before Huong was finishing the night shift. He told her that he wouldn't be coming back to the hotel until nine o'clock that evening. He asked her to take his passport and key — not to lock them up on the other side of the counter but to carry them with her to her home. "I'm gonna be in the city for the whole day," he said. "That's why I want you to have this stuff — my key especially. You can't let me come back early."

She laughed. "You are asking me to come to your room later?" She winked at the other concierge.

"Today, I'm going to get by on four dollars!" He took out the bills and waved them in her face.

"Okay, Okay. Good luck to you," Huong said, gently gesturing him away from her.

He thrust the money in her face again. "Just the four dollars, Huong. I can do this." He took a step back, suddenly conscious of his obnoxiousness, but not really caring much either. "Do you think you could write the hotel address on my arm? I'm a little worried about getting lost."

"Sure thing, sweetie." With other tourists filing past, Huong bent over and wrote on him. "Don't sweat too much, sweetie. This may come off in the sun."

"I'm not coming back until tonight," he said.

"Yeah, good luck," Huong said, but not very convincingly.

He set off on his one-day excursion through the streets of Saigon. He walked past the motorized rickshaw drivers, who paid little attention to him. He walked past the motorcycle shops, past the vendors that sold lychees, and stopped in the market place for breakfast. With a budget for the day in mind, he asked Thanh Ha for some fruit. She gave him an apple and a mango. In the same way as he might hold a poker hand, he thrust the four bills in front of her. She took three of his dollars and he walked away.

He did not acknowledge his rage until he'd walked a full block south through the market. Thanh Ha, the tempestuous lady who had served him his meals over much of the week, and whom he'd fantasized about every night, had chosen this, his second last day in town, to rip him off. She'd stripped him of three of his bills, three-quarters of his self-prescribed quota for the day. *How dare she take advantage of me like that!*

His walk through the streets that morning was tarnished for two reasons: he was hungry — the fruit hadn't dissipated his hunger — and he was obsessed with the outrageousness of the incident, which by then had transformed into an intolerable deceit. He walked along a wide boulevard with his head down. He forced himself to look up when he passed the Giac Lam Pagoda with its carved jackwood statues. The Vietnamese are supposed to be honest, he thought. He stood for an hour watching water puppetry on a man-made pond. He stared at a man gutting tiny fish flapping on a wagon. He wanted to visit the Phu Tho Natural Institute of Technology, but he had no idea if he was in the right district and he didn't feel like asking, nor did he feel like getting into a cab. *I know she's poor, but I worked hard myself to come here. It's not my fault a planned economy messed up the Vietnamese for over thirty years. It's not my fault the French colonized the area. It's not my fault I'm rich and she's poor.* He reached into his pocket from time to time to ensure that the one remaining bill was still there. The money was moist from his perspiration.

At five o'clock, he took another stab at buying food. He was hungry, yet determined not to make the same mistake twice. He pointed to the noodle soup and said, "Half a dollar."

The old lady countered in halting English that the price of a bowl of soup was one dollar. Unwilling to concede defeat, he haggled and then stomped off, only to return a few minutes later.

"One dollar," she said. "One dollar."

"No, I'm not paying that much. For a dollar you can give me some of those spring rolls."

"I am sorry," she said. "I can't give you any food."

"You've been a great help," he said. He moved on to another merchant, who was unwilling to even talk to him.

He walked to another market a few streets away, where he finally found someone who'd accept his price. He was worried that the merchants from the previous market would follow him in an attempt to dissuade this man from co-operating. The man served his soup and, in a grand act of conciliation, handed him two thousand dong (which Russell would later learn was worth about fifteen cents).

Tired from the exertion of his adventure, Russell made it back to the hotel just as Huong was starting her evening shift. He was carrying two bags of McDonald's, a two-litre bottle of Pepsi and a pineapple.

"Where did you get the money to buy that?" she said.

"I succumbed to hunger, I guess. I had some extra money stashed in my sock."

He stood at his window and looked down at the neighbourhood. By two o'clock in the morning all activity in the neighbourhood had ceased. What a wonderful holiday, thought Russell. Nobody, not Mom or Dad, not Ray — he'd try to explain — but nobody would fully understand his experiences. The funny cab ride. The guy could have robbed him. Huong. Thanh Ha and her family. The beautiful Pagoda he visited. The district was hilarious. Or was that the right word? Nobody else had access to these impressions. And that was because they were *his*. He'd have to thank his mother. She'd been right all along. This had been a fantastic idea. He also wanted to thank Huong for her kindness. Maybe right now. But no, she'd think it strange at three in the morning.

He woke up after only a few hours of sleep and packed his suitcase for the flight. He separated the little Canadian pins into two separate stacks and gave one pile to Huong, who said, "Thanks. That's really nice of you." When he was at the elevator, she added, "Come back next year." He didn't turn around. He knew that she'd meant this. That she probably didn't say this to every customer.

He headed to the market and left the second pile on Thanh Ha's steel kitchen. Nobody was awake, so he was able to sneak back to the hotel without being seen.

He was anxious when passing through immigration at the airport — two tough-looking Vietnamese were carrying rifles at the checkout area — but was surprised when he opened his passport. A yellow post-it note was stuck to his photo. *I guessed when I first met you that you were probably born here. This is a beautiful place, no? I hope you learned about your ancestry. Come back some time for another visit. I'll find you a nice Vietnamese wife. — Huong*

TOM AND WILKIE

WILKIE SEES AN ELDERLY MAN BESIDE A run-down barbecue shack, next to the town's community centre, looking out at the graveyard, his withering grey hair messed by the wind. He is seven years younger than Wilkie, but at seventy, old in comparison to most everyone else. His name is Tom. He's still handsome, his jaw and shoulders manly and sturdy, whereas Wilkie lost his looks in his early thirties, if he ever had any. The muscles around Tom's mouth are twitching. His wife's funeral was earlier today so he's grieving. He'd be surprised to learn that Wilkie is watching him, as he would also be shocked that Wilkie has observed him for the past fifty-five or so years. Tom underestimated Wilkie early on, dismissed him as someone of no consequence. Wilkie is Robert Wilkinson, owner of O'Brien's Restaurant and president of the Harriers, a men's group dedicated to the survival of the town. His ancestors, Scottish and English, have been involved in the Harriers for generations.

When he was a teenager Wilkie was an assistant coach of the local hockey team because his father was head coach and because he loved being around hockey players, even if they were young. And Tom was simply the best bantam hockey player to play the game. Wilkie's dad had him pegged as someone who might make it as a hockey player and then return to become a community leader and contribute to the economic wellbeing of their bucolic, non-descript tobacco town, population 1800, two hours south of Toronto.

A doughnut shop, a water tower, a gas station, a diner and a grocery store surrounded three industrial buildings of terracotta brick. There was a suburb to the north of Main Street and one to the south, both filled with bungalows and two-story residences. There was a nine-hole golf course. After that, tobacco farms extended for miles.

Tom was only in grade three when Wilkie's father and other business people in the area financed a brick community centre on the periphery of town, just south of the graveyard, but as soon as it was built he was easily gliding around the slower skating Denton Bears and potting goal after goal. The Bears' coach, a purple-faced man with slits for eyes, said, "You take it easy on us today, Tommy." The boy, barely smiling, said, "You better put eight players on the ice then," and winked at his right-winger, Sammy Belinski. He was cocky for someone his age, but boy could he play! The referee, a retired police officer from the Davisville and Highway 54 intersection, acknowledged his greatness by grabbing his chinstrap and giving it a tug. Mothers from Denton smiled at Tom as he lumbered gracefully to the dressing room after the game.

Tom combed his black hair to the left. His eyes were the same colour as wood stain. He'd sneak into the arena Saturday nights and stand in the middle of the rink looking in awe at the colossal space, weighing his feelings of importance against his insignificance in the huge rink. At these moments, he believed that the community centre with the new red brick, clean boards and modern canteen, epitomized the greatness of the town.

One day, on the road to an afternoon game against Sutton, Tom was studying the map in his father's car, the roads leading in and out of town. He asked his father geographical and historical questions then became quiet as the flat countryside changed to rolling hills, from tobacco to soybeans. He was disparaging of Sutton's arena, a sign that he was due for a productive afternoon. His confidence depended on the size of an opposing team's arena. When he played in an arena that was bigger, his confidence would suffer. Before this game, Tom watched the Yellow Jackets get out of their parents' cars, and mingle in the canteen. Listening to the farm boys chatter, he was surprised and baffled that they talked about the Leafs — other kids in other towns loved all the same things he did!

After the game Wilkie sharpened skates and put the goalie equipment away, and then his dad dropped him off at O'Brien's — his busboy shift was to start soon. Tom's family came in two hours later for dinner, during which Tom's father described each of Tom's goals as the boy struggled to fit his mouth over his cheeseburger. Wilkie served Tom a piece of chocolate cake. Tom would surely appreciate his generosity of spirit. "He's good, Jim, your boy," he said to Tom's father.

One summer the town hosted a Saturday evening dance. Young Tom and Sammy Belinski ran onto the concrete floor and slid under tables. Adults sat on lawn chairs and fanned themselves in the heat. Teenagers drank beer out of Styrofoam cups at the back of the arena. Tom and Sammy Belinski and Tom's younger sister lowered themselves under the concrete stands. Surrounded by cobwebs and dirt, they scavenged for bottles and loose change dropped from the stands. Afterward,

Tom walked home with his family. "Mr. James showed up in his tractor," he said, "and parked it right in there with the cars." His father said, "Old Wilson sure can eat hot-dogs. Did you see how many hot-dogs he ate?" His mother said, "Karen was in a good mood tonight. She's got absolute control over her kids. There's no doubt about that."

Eight years later, Tom had black fuzz on his lip and no longer dominated games. Bigger kids from farm areas grabbed and held him, hindering him from sliding in on opposing goalies. Finesse players from London used their sticks to strip him of the puck and chop at his ankles. Wilkie's dad was dismayed that Tom did not retaliate. It was during this season, in the canteen after a game against Bowan, that Wilkie overheard his father tell Mr. Belinski, his latest assistant, that Tom would never play Junior A hockey, nor Junior B for that matter.

Tom's enthusiasm for the game did wane. The stench of equipment and the drama in the stands dulled him. The arena was as uninspiring and unimaginative as the endless fields of tobacco. He went through the motions on the ice, making no extra effort. Only sheer talent allowed him to score an occasional goal.

On a desolate Friday afternoon in the middle of the winter, Tom was sitting with his friends in O'Brien's. He flicked a penny at Wilkie's back as Wilkie made his way to another table. Pennies clanked off tables and left dents in pictures. They'd polished off two mickeys of vodka at Faldo's, the nine-hole golf course, and they waited for Wilkie to turn the corner to serve non-smoking customers, and then looted the potato chip display. Under the table Tom distributed three of the bags. The sight of Wilkie, a twenty-four year old man, yelling at him and out of control (the flicked pennies must have stung), left him feeling smug and superior.

That summer, with his hair long in the back, and still without acne, Tom sauntered into the arena with a pretty girl. A little boy's head emerged from under a table. He palmed the kid's head and stuffed it back, moved around the table, end to end, blocking the kid's exit, until the boy was stifling sobs. Tom smirked. "You a little girl?" He joined his girlfriend and others at the back of the arena. "Mr. James is a strange bugger," he said. "He drives his tractor into town even though he has a car." Sammy Belinski said, "That old man Mr. Wilson sure can eat hot-dogs. He's putting them back faster than a pig would eat." Tom's girlfriend said, "Mrs. Porter is a rag with her kids."

Late on this hot July evening, with everybody dancing and with his girl at his side, some of the derisiveness washed away. On his way out the scarred arena doors Tom said, "This town's kinda nice."

Two years later Tom waited long after his parents had left the party, this time a winter festival, and then walked down the slushy streets with Sammy Belinski. "I'm going to strap a bomb to myself," he said, "and climb the water tower and light myself up, and drown the middle of this piss-ass town." Belinski thought this was funny so he told Shauna Maples.

Wilkie was shoveling his driveway when Shauna and her friends came by, her pert seventeen-year-old figure illuminated in the dark. They may have been smoking dope because they were giggling a lot. "Hey Wilkie," she said. "You'd better fill your sink with water. Tom's going to blow the tower up."

Wilkie went to Tom's father's kitchen door the next morning and told him what he'd heard, and later that week Jim arranged for Tom to spend a week in Toronto. Tom stayed at an apartment owned by one of Jim's customers who had flown west for the March break. When he returned after four days he had wounded eyes, and seemed a softer version of himself. His family took him and Sammy Belinski to O'Brien's. Sammy Belinski listened with rapt attention as Tom cowered in the booth, recalling his stay in Toronto.

After everyone had eaten, Tom cleared the table of dirty dishes and carried them into the kitchen. "Thanks a lot, Wilkie," he said. Outside in the falling snow, he grabbed his mother's arm to prevent her from falling on the ice. His mother, who had never been an affectionate lady, looked puzzled.

The next day he came back to O'Brien's, sat in a booth, put his face in his hands, and said, "Toronto is filthy. Nobody there is like you or me. No one speaks English. At first I loved to take the subway and bus around the city, but after a while I hated it because I had to sit beside people who stank. It was like I was the freak. Just cause I was tidy and normal! Apartments there have thousands of people in them and not one person says hello to anybody. I stayed on the tenth floor of a large building and it wasn't until the third day that I saw anyone. You know what? For all the people there, it's a building full of ghosts. People live there but they don't come out, you know what I mean?"

Wilkie poured him a cup of coffee. "When I was there," he said. "I saw a homeless man in a tent on the sidewalk. I woke up one morning and I saw the guy behind a building — get this — he was taking a shit. It was the strangest thing I ever saw." He slapped the bar and laughed.

"It is impossible to have any type of true friendship there," Tom said. "You go out for a walk and then you come home alone. There's no sense of community. Everybody there is shallow. They judge you by how much money you have."

Tom's car dealership — the business he took over after his father retired — thrived and Tom purchased a two-story house just south of Main Street. Sammy Belinski played pickup hockey on Saturday evenings. He tried to recruit Tom, now slightly balding and with a four-year old, a three-year old, and a two-month old, to play with them, but Tom refused. He was too important to play a child's game, after all. *Who wears hockey equipment?* Shin pads, garter belts, hockey socks and jock-cups were all things from his childhood. Tom ballooned in weight and his face reddened. He enrolled his children in the local league.

One January day, while in the canteen with his oldest son's team and the rest of the parents, he refused to buy a second hot-dog for his son. He watched in admiration as his son made the rounds of three of the more vulnerable kids on the team, convincing each of them to relinquish fifty cents. He watched his kid strut to the canteen window to buy the hotdog and Coke. His kid bit off part of the hotdog, doused the cross-section with ketchup and then tore into another piece. He recognized the smirk on his son's face as he ate his hot-dog and drank his Coke.

His son's talent on the ice was less obvious than Tom's had been. The boy wasn't particularly fast or large. Tom, however, claimed that his son's hockey prowess, while not supported by statistics, was nevertheless evident in an intangible way.

Tom and his friends bought tickets to a Saturday evening Leafs game in Toronto — the Penguins were paying a visit. Tom noticed Wilkie in the back seat, and snarled at Sammy, who'd invited him at the last minute. On Highway 401, Tom talked incessantly of the week he'd spent as a youth in Toronto. He peppered Sammy with questions about present-day Toronto, combining his questions with comments that seemed to disparage the city and yet also hold it in awe.

At O'Brien's the next evening, he was quiet. It was busy, so Wilkie couldn't talk with the guys that much but made a point of being nice to Tom, looking for a return to the honesty that had connected them that one moment forty years earlier. Tom's wife, Melinda said, "Why are you so strange around Wilkie?"

His large body slouched.

Now with a bulbous nose and grey-speckled moustache, Tom walked into the community centre. A group of five teenagers sat in the stands surreptitiously smoking dope. Tom said to Belinski, "I got a bitch of a sunburn on my back last Sunday, Sam. Todd got three runs. One was in the ninth that tied the score. I had to take off my shirt to wave the boy in on his second and forgot to put it back on. Where were you? You could have come over for my steaks. I just got some from St. Mary's my very self. They're 'bout the tenderest pieces of meat you ever tasted."

"We just had our second grandkid, Tom," Sam said. "We were down in Ilderton waiting for baby Stephanie to come. She arrived just past ten o'clock. She's got a little birthmark on her neck. You should see her."

"Next time bring her for the steaks. We'll cut one up small. She can watch Todd play this Thursday and, tell you what, I'll put some of that meat in a blender and give her a straw so she can start off proper. You hear that CEB, that tobacco company, is coming to town — gonna transform our place . . . "

"You know, Tom," Sam said. "Wilkie's representing the Harriers. Wilkie invited CEB here to open their branch warehouse."

When the CEB businessmen came to town in a limousine, Tom wore his best checkered suit, and loitered on Main Street.

Wilkie and his brother escorted the CEB officials to O'Brien's for lunch. On the way into the restaurant his brother said, "Should we introduce Tom to these guys? There aren't too many businesses still around, and Tom's dealership is still operational, barely."

"Can't do that," Wilkie said. "Tom might open his mouth."

He was desperately hoping CEB would plant their seed in the small town, but his hopes were off by 300 km. Their decision to set up elsewhere precipitated the relocation of two other tobacco-related businesses. Sammy Belinski took a job in a big company and moved to Kitchener-Waterloo. Tom's wife died of cancer. Today was the funeral.

Afterwards, Tom came to O'Brien's and sat in a booth.

"You used to be the Knight's best player," Wilkie said. "You had a knack for scoring goals that I don't see in any of the kids these days."

Tom drawled, "They don't even play hockey much anymore. Summer dances are gone. Yard sales have replaced them and even then only once in a blue moon. This town's got no more young people. What's left for old guys like us, Wilkie?"

"Do you feel like joining the Harriers, Tom? We need members."

"I don't know. That's not really my interest," he said.

"I kinda feel like me and the Harriers have let the town down," said Wilkie. "We haven't realized our potential, have we?"

"Not your fault, Wilkie. You've done your bit. It's a losing cause."

"Whatever happened in Toronto, Tom? When you went there all those years ago?"

"Oh, that," said Tom. "Yeah, I was young and stupid then. It was nothing really. I went into this coffee shop and there was this girl and this boy and they looked nice enough so I told them about how I'd scored all those goals in bantam league and about how I was a star hockey player, and then I told them I was feeling left out in Toronto and how I was looking for fun and so at some point I noticed that this guy, this city guy, was just talking to this girl and he wasn't listening to anything I was saying. So I went back to my table and sat there and stared at them for a while but they didn't even try to talk to me, you know, to smooth things over and so I left and came back here because people there seemed so unfriendly. That was all."

Tom left O'Brien's. He walked past the water tower and shuddered. He walked past the decrepit arena and had an inclination to get a hot chocolate, but the arena was empty and would be torn down soon. The winter snow had been too much for the rafters to support and the building was considered dangerous. He entered and walked over to the concrete stands. As a child he'd looked for bottles and loose change. He sat in the stands and looked at the rink paved with cement. He left the building and walked to the front of the rotted barbecue hut.

He's still thinking about his dead wife. He's also thinking about Mr. James and the tractor he drove to town, about all the hot-dogs consumed by old Mr. Wilson, and Karen Porter's sharp tongue. The countless burgers he ate as a child. He looks out across the interminable fields of tobacco. His eyes rest on the graveyard north of the arena. He looks at the town graveyard, and comes to the realization that he along with Wilkie and the rest of the geriatric population will soon be buried there.

The Revisionist

Jim stepped onto the subway car, briefly looked at the TTC map above the doors and then, to no one in particular, he said, "Is this going to Pape?" The only passengers within hearing distance were two elderly Chinese women, who stared ahead and continued to speak in Mandarin. Jim looked at them grumpily and made his way to the rear of the subway car. He felt tense. His neck was so rigid he had to swivel his entire body to look right or left.

He spotted an attractive woman who was wearing a business suit and sidled up to her. The woman, in her mid-twenties, held an *Elle* magazine in front of her face. "This is the first time that I've ever worn a tie," he said. He rubbed the white bone-hard scar on his cheek.

The woman winced. "Oh," she said, returning her gaze back to the magazine she was reading.

"This is the first time that I've ever worn a tie."

"What did you say?"

He wagged his bony index finger at her. "God-awful thing feels weird. I own my own roofing business, so obviously I don't wear it while I'm on the roof, though I don't get up there much anymore because we've expanded and I'm mostly in the office these days."

The woman frowned and looked anxiously at the other passengers. She put her magazine down and stared straight ahead.

"I like to get up there sometimes just to show the men that I can still haul tiles with the best of them."

"Excuse me, I have to get off."

"My wife is waiting for me back home. I mean — she's waiting to see how things go for me at the bank. I have to go to the bank first and then I'm going to call her and tell her how things went." Jim held a yellow document up and was about to explain further when the woman got up and walked to the doors at the other end.

"I've got three of the Leafs. Anybody need a card? I've got just about every card. I'll trade for gobstoppers." I turned to one of the shorter boys in line and said, "Hey big guy, do you want Daryl Sittler? I've got two of him."

Lanny, a really big guy, walked to the front of the line. He had dark, straight hair that was feathered at the sides. I was waiting with everyone else to get onto the court. He barged past us like we were third-graders. "I was king at the end of last recess," he said, "and so I get to be it again." He grabbed the large rubber ball from a shy little guy, who looked pissed but didn't say anything.

Patricia, a cute girl with cheeks like hamburger buns and blue eyes the same colour as the marker we used in art, watched us from the baseball diamond.

Lanny had a lot of nerve to think he could be king two recesses in a row. "Who does he think he is?" I said. "Does he think he's in charge of us? How can he just butt in like that?"

Inside the bank Jim was bewildered. He didn't know what to do. He walked cautiously to the back of a line and asked, "Does anyone here know where I can get a mortgage?"

A lady in line pointed at some chairs in the corner near some plants and said, "Over there, I think."

"Thank you, ma'am."

As he neared the chairs he brushed the stringy blond hair out of his eyes. Once seated in front of a potted fern, he wagged his finger at a man next to him. "What rate are you getting, boss?"

The balding man had a touch of auburn hair around his ears. His face was swollen and red. He said, "What do you mean?"

"What's the bank giving you? What interest rate are they offering?" Jim tapped the balding man on the shoulder with his knuckles. "Banks make all this money by doing nothing. They don't build anything. They don't help anyone. At least doctors and cops are around to serve the public. Bankers have it nice. It's easy money for them. They just sit back and take it all in."

"Yeah, look at these people," the man said, pointing to a clerk. "Sitting on their stools — counting their money."

"You don't know a lot about anything, do you?" Jim said gruffly. He addressed the woman next to the balding man. "Big guy, here, has no idea of the workings of big banks. I've got no beef with the front line staff. These folks at the counters are busy. They're counting money. Actually doing something. But do you think these folks get any of the money they count? No way. They make a pittance. It's the fat cats lolling about behind those doors over there that do all the damage. Well, I've got something in store for them. They think they've got my business all sewn up, but I've got a card up my sleeve." The woman had turned her back and was ignoring him.

"I hear interest rates are going up soon," the balding man said, in a way to redeem himself.

Jim slapped him on the shoulder and said, "Tell you what, boss — you let me go before you and when I'm finished getting my deal, I'll hook you up with a decent rate. After today they'll have had their fill of me, that's for certain."

The snow had melted. There was a lot of gravel on the ground. Lanny grabbed the red ball, walked over to me and said, "What are you going to do about it?" He pushed me with the ball. "You think you're a businessman because you trade hockey cards. That's a laugh! You're a loser." Lanny took a step closer and bumped me again with the rubber ball. The ground was slippery because of all the gravel. If I fell I might seriously hurt myself. The pebbles might get under my skin and cause an infection. The doctors at Scarborough General would have to do surgery on my cheek and I didn't want that, right?

I started to push back. Lanny shifted his weight and pulled hard on the ball. I tripped over his foot and fell. I was going to fall face first on the ground. I was about to scrape my face on the gravel. Time slowed and I was suspended in air. My body shuddered. My limbs strained and my skin was being stretched for an alien takeover. At the last second I stuck out my skinny arm, which was suddenly strong, strong enough, in fact, to bench press four plates at Gold's. When I got to my feet, my arm was scraped and bleeding, but it wasn't broken.

"Are you okay, Jimmy?" Patricia yelled from the diamond.

The bank manager extended his hand to Jim, who was staring blankly ahead. They shook hands. "You can come with me, sir."

"It's my pleasure," Jim said.

The bank manager led him into a room and said, "Have a seat. How can I help you?"

"I thought you people would have plush leather sofas in your offices. And those flat-screen TVs."

"Well, I might not get much done then, right?" The bank manager laughed good-naturedly. "How can I help you?"

The bank manager's navy suit hung perfectly from his broad shoulders. Jim felt inadequate in his shirt and tie. "Look boss, I want to know what your best rate is." He lightly touched his scar.

The manager told him.

"You can do better than that, boss." He smiled coyly. "Give me something we can work with. You're not even trying."

"That's all I can offer. Our rates are competitive."

"The sensible thing would be to consult with your boss. Can you talk to him about getting me a better rate?"

"It's pretty much a standard rate. We have some room for negotiations for larger properties, but this is the best offer that I can give you today."

Jim noticed the absence of a wedding ring. "Are you married, boss? Do you have a wife and kids?" He felt his face quiver. "I've got a wife and kids."

The bank manager's phone rang. "I have to take this call," he said.

Jim stared at the crumpled yellow sheet that he held in his hand.

"You sure you want to do that, big guy?" I took a step toward Lanny and placed my hand on his forearm. "The good Lord," I said, "has made it clear that one of us is going to be scarred today. May as well be you and not me."

Because my arms and legs were bulging under my skin and because my voice had changed, Patricia and the other little guys were looking at me strangely. My frame had the power of someone who'd hauled over a thousand kilos of tile. I grabbed Lanny's arm and whipped him around like a rag doll. His legs buckled and he dropped. I pinned his wrist to the ground with my left knee. I grabbed the back of his head and jammed his face remorselessly into the gravel, grating his cheek on the pebbles. Lanny howled in pain but I continued to grate his face like cheese. Blood spurted, shaking in large droplets from his shredded cheek. Blood was staining the gravel surface when I finally released my grip. Lanny coiled into a fetal position and blubbered like the little coward that he was.

Mr. Katz, the senior gym teacher, stuck his face through the crowd. At this point I was kicking Lanny in the ribs. "Lanny had it coming," Mr. Katz said. "Under similar circumstances Lanny wouldn't have given Jimmy any mercy." The other kids were laughing and celebrating because Lanny was due for a licking — many of 'em wished that they were kicking the snot out of Lanny and not me. I was a ferocious fighter for my age. Patricia and the other boys cheered as if I were a hero.

"If you think you've got me beat," Jim said, "you've clearly got another think coming. Take a look at this." He held the yellow dog-eared document in front of him. "I've got 3.2 per cent from Loblaws. Loblaws supports the underdog. The president is in my corner."

My body shuddered again, as if a ghost had left it and I was again just an innocent, harmless twelve-year-old.

Patricia thought that I was handsome. She saw that I wasn't going to be scarred and that Lanny, who'd started the whole thing, was going to have a hideous scar. He was going to be disfigured for life. Patricia saw my potential. She saw the man that I'd become. She knew that I'd one day graduate from Seneca College and that I'd own my own roofing business and that I'd get married and have two little guys and my own house as well.

"You just lost my business. Go ahead and keep the piece of paper, boss. I've got more copies at home and another copy stashed away in a safe, private location." Jim's scar was itchy, so he scratched it. On the way out he yelled, "Go to Loblaws for your money. This place is a rip off!"

Everyone turned to watch him storm across the floor to the double doors leading to the street. He was in a hurry. He wanted to try the Royal Bank on Logan Street before it closed at five o'clock.

SHALLOWNESS

To: Rebecca (rebeccabrown88@gmail.com)
From: Jean
Cc:
Re: your replacement

I haven't had the best week. I'm pretty sure I'm going to get fired because of the girl who replaced you. This new girl is something else.

She applies layers of rouge, coats her eyebrows and lashes with Maybelline and somehow perks up her breasts and buttocks. She wears garish earrings. The only accessory I have is a headband, and I strap this on only when I want to dress up. I think you're the only other woman that could wear blue jeans to work and not give a rat's ass.

There's a fog of perfume that hovers over her desk. She hung a fuzzy pink Hello Kitty doll on the wall of your old cubicle. I told her this was sacrilegious to your memory and not really appropriate for an office. She whined that it gave her luck. She flaunts the fact that she's a size two. She laughed when I told her that her waist was the same size as my thigh.

She doesn't have an original thought in her head. She's giddy about *Will and Grace*. She idolizes *Ally McBeal*. I was discussing the latest Alberto Salazar film a few days back. I looked over and I saw her puzzled look of incomprehension. In fact, she's probably unacquainted with all foreign films. (Who do I have to talk to around here now that you've left?)

She idly stands around other people's desks at lunch. She reeks of phoniness. She reads Steve his horoscope every day — like he gives a flying f . . . A client was waiting for her at her cubicle and she raised her finger and continued to gab on the phone. So I said to the client, "Samantha's just sorting out her plans for Friday night. Maybe I can help you?" I tell you, if I don't get fired, and if this is how she conducts business I'm going to have a busy year.

She showed up at the pub two days ago and hugged everyone. Such phony affection. In the middle of the evening she started to dance seductively in the aisle of the pub. Know what I did? I stood up and jiggled next to her. People laughed.

Miss Samantha had no idea what I was up to. After the song she spouted platitudes about how funny she thought we were together. I'd drunk about five beers and was tired of her affected camaraderie. "We're not friends," I said, "so why act as if we are? Why spend valuable time getting to know each other when we don't really care?" Then I gave her the goods. "Look," I said. "I pride myself in being an honest person, so I might as well give you a head's up. I was making fun of you back there when I was dancing with you."

Her reply? She said, "What end does it serve you to ridicule me. Up until now I've seen you as a moody but funny person. I've liked listening to your stories and I've appreciated your sense of humour. Now I'm always going to be careful around you." She gave me this Prince Myshkin look — a guileless stare that was empty of irony.

I took a long swig of my beer and said, "Listen, Samantha. You're obviously so shallow that you don't get it. I'm my own person and if people don't like me so be it. I'm not going to change. Why should I suffer fools?" And I cackled, but she had it coming, don't you think?

The poor little thing choked back a few tears and left the bar.

She obviously was going to tell all our colleagues, so I beat her to the punch. I approached each and every person that night and told my side of the story. I asked Steve to meet me outside. I told him he's got to get rid of her — either that or I might not come back to work. He said he'd look into it. I'll bet you any money she's complained to him about me and is scheming to get me fired.

If only you were here. You'd take my side. Sometimes I think we're the only truly genuine people on this planet. How's your new job? I'd love to hear from you. I haven't heard from you since you left?!?

xoxox

Jean

INERTIA

I LIE IN BED FOR AN HOUR listening to 102.1, "The Edge." Eventually, I get up and open the kitchen window. I take a bowl from the cupboard and fill it with corn flakes. There's no milk so I eat the cereal with my fingers, then lie on the sofa and turn on the television. I flick for a while and then stop at a middle-aged woman doing yoga. She's a little thick in the hips, but with leotards she's got the legs of a twenty-year old. I light up, and take a drag from a joint. I watch the woman and stroke myself, but give it up after my prick goes limp.

A George Brown College pamphlet is open on the coffee table beside me. A few of the business courses on the page are highlighted in yellow, though not by me. My dad brought it over the other day and told me that I should take a look, which was strange because we haven't spoken much the last two years. I thought he'd given up hope when I was eighteen and moved in with Rudy. It's easy living here. Rudy's the superintendent. It's his father's building. I guess I should be paying a little rent, but Rudy hasn't mentioned that I'm here to his father, so I haven't paid a cent. Instead I supply Rudy with weed. Lots of it. I buy it with the money I earn from working at a gas station in the west end of Toronto. Whenever he smokes up, I smoke up as well. I don't want to be rude, right? We've been smoking up every other day for six years straight. It was good for the first five years, but lately I've been wondering if there isn't more to life.

There's a thud on the other side of the wall.

I step over a bag full of Kentucky Fried Chicken bones and open the door to the third-floor hallway. A teenaged boy is sitting cross-legged, his back against the wall, long black bangs hanging in front of his face so I can't see his eyes. Why doesn't he comb that mess? Equally repulsive is the fuzz on his upper lip. I'd like to hold him down and shave it off. He holds an Apple magazine inches from his eyes. His limbs are skinny, like a doll's. "This one's got a camera connector," he says.

"Hey little man," I say. "What's your name?"

"Joseph. What's yours?"

"Ben. Where you from?"

"The Philippines."

"Why don't you be on your way?"

"What do you mean?"

"Go on and be with your own. With your mom and dad. Rudy and I don't like visitors too much."

"Rudy? I met Rudy," the kid says. "He's gonna help me earn a bit of cash."

"He is?" I'm aware of how surprised I sound.

A week later, while I'm watching *Judge Judy*, I hear people talking just outside the door. I put on some shorts and open it. Joseph is scrubbing the scuffed hallway floor. Rudy's looming over him. The girls at our high school used to love his long hair. They wouldn't find him so attractive anymore.

He's pot-bellied, with a perpetual leering expression on his face, and now his hair is greasy. "Put some weight into that, Joseph," he says.

"I'm not sure the black marks will come off," Joseph says.

"Sure they will." Rudy winks at me. "Every mark has to come off. You told me you wanted some work and then you complain when I give it to you."

Joseph's head bobs up and down in concentration. Drops of his sweat trickle to the floor. "I'm not complaining." He squats on his heels, swinging like a metronome from side to side, chipping away at gum and unidentifiable grunge with a scraper. His wiry arms stretch to get at bits in the corner. He reaches into a bucket for a sponge that drips black water down his arm. He coats the floor with water from his sponge, mops up the loosened scraps, and then flips the muddy, stringy muck into a plastic bag.

When Rudy goes into our apartment, Joseph cranes his neck, making eye contact with me, and says, "He just wants me to do a professional job. He might give me more work at the other buildings on our block." He smiles shyly.

"The other buildings are even harder to clean," I say. "You and your parents should have moved somewhere else." I can tell I've hurt his feelings. He doesn't look up when I say, "See ya."

I'm awake. My brain's a little sluggish, but I can see that my dad's in the room. I feel his smallness. He has a slight build, a thin, quivering moustache, and sad, blue eyes. A glass of water's in his hand. Oh fuck. There's a smouldering roach on the table. Can he smell it? "Hey, Dad," I say. "How'd you get in here?"

"Rudy, let me in," he says.

I sit up. Rudy's in the wicker chair in the corner of the room, smoking a cigarette. At least it's not dope. "Is Ben late for his 8:30 appointment on Bay Street, Mr. Wilson?"

"I wouldn't know about that, Rudy," my dad says.

"What tie are you going to wear for that meeting, Ben?"

"Shut up, Rudy," I say. "How long have you been here, Dad?"

"I just got here," he says. His voice sounds depressed. He's not even acting like everything's okay. "I came by to see if you've filled in the registration form for George Brown. The last day to register is in two weeks."

"Ben and I are thinking about selling our shares. Is it a good time to sell now, Mr. Wilson?"

"I wouldn't know about that, Rudy," my dad says.

"Stop it, Rudy," I say. "I'll fill it out soon, Dad. Just give me some time."

"All right," he says. He hands me the glass of water. "You can stay at home for free when you're at George Brown."

I don't know what to say. Before I can thank him, Rudy says, "Will any of those business courses Ben's taking help him understand the elasticity of the weed market, Mr. Wilson?"

When he leaves I curl up as small as I can on the sofa. It's not what he's said. It was nice of him to offer to let me stay at his place. It's not even what Rudy's said. I feel shitty because of what my dad hasn't said. No complaint about the weed, whatsoever. Is this a new normal?

Three days have gone by since my father's visit. I get off the elevator with milk, bread and rolling papers from the 7-Eleven. Joseph is talking to Rudy by the stairwell. "It took me about five hours to clean all six floors," he says. "If you give me ten dollars, it means I worked for two dollars an hour." He reminds me of the boy in the Charles Dickens story who says, "Please sir, can I have some more?"

"You can complain, but I'm only giving you ten bucks," Rudy says. "I don't know how people do business in the Philippines. You should've asked how much I'd give you before you started. It's too late now."

Joseph reluctantly takes the bill from Rudy's hand.

"The first floor is scuffed by the main entrance," Rudy says. "It looks horrible."

"That's because people walked on it while it was still wet."

"That isn't my problem. The agreement was that you'd do a good job. You said that, didn't you?"

"I'll get my sponge and fix it."

"You do that." Rudy gets in the elevator and it descends.

Joseph smiles at me with forced cheerfulness.

"Why are you taking his shit?" I ask.

"What do you mean?"

"Why not pour some dirty water on his floor. Piss in his mailbox."

"Why? I thought you guys were friends?"

"Go and finish the fucking job, Joseph." I'm shaking, so I go into the apartment and lie down on the sofa. That I'm full of so much hate doesn't make sense. My dad's never spoken badly about anyone, not black guys or Chinese guys. He always got mad as hell when Rudy told a gay or racist joke. As for me, I'm not overly fond of brown or Chinese dudes, but Rudy's worse — he's a racist asshole. When he tells a joke I always laugh, but lately I've felt like he's wandered too far toward the Hate. I want to at least keep an open mind about things.

Someone's knocking at the door.

"Can you get that?" Rudy yells from the washroom, where he's taking a bath.

I pinch out the roach I'm smoking, examine my grey sweatpants and T-shirt for anything gross, and then open the door. Joseph's staring at me with a smile on his face. I haven't seen him for a few weeks. "I'm collecting beer bottles. If you want I can go to the beer store and return them for you. We can share the refund."

"Looking to make a buck, are you?"

Joseph's smile widens. "Yes, sir."

"All right. Just hold on a second. There's twelve bottles in the kitchen."

When I return, Rudy, in his bathrobe, is in the doorway bumping his belly against Joseph's duffel bag. He's dropping jars of congealed mayonnaise and Cheese Whiz in with the beer bottles.

"I can't get any money for these," Joseph says. "I just want beer bottles."

"What?" Rudy says. "You'll take my beer bottles and not my other glass containers? What kind of service are you providing? All you have to do is put them in the blue box out front."

Joseph's smile disappears but he's going to do what Rudy wants. He pulls the duffel bag, so full of bottles that it can't be zipped up, onto his shoulder. Tepid beer spills from a bottle onto the boy's shirt. A dill pickle jar rolls to the side of the bag, totters and then, in what seems like slow motion, drops to the floor and shatters.

Joseph says, "Shit," then lowers the duffel bag and says to Rudy, "I'll clean that up after I get back."

"Do it before you go," Rudy says. "The glass might cut someone."

In spite of the smile, it's easy to see that Joseph's pissed off.

"Don't look at me like that," Rudy says. "You smashed the jar." And then, more quietly, "Impudent little fuck."

Joseph gets a broom from his apartment and sweeps up the glass. He removes some of the bottles and puts them in a plastic bag. He lugs the duffel bag in his arms down the stairs and comes back for the remaining bottles. I stand at the window, eating stale pretzels, watching Joseph on Queen Street. Every ten metres or so he puts down one bag, and goes back for the other.

When he reappears on the street with his empty duffel, I hustle down to meet him in the lobby. "You didn't need to take his recyclables. He shouldn't have asked you to do that."

"He isn't all bad," Joseph says. "He let me go door-to-door and ask everyone for bottles. He didn't have to let me do that. Thanks for giving me your bottles, mister. Here's your half." He drops sixty cents into my hand, smiling. "See you later."

I wasn't always so useless. My dad's a high school geography teacher. He helped me with my homework. I got nothing but As and Bs in grades nine and ten. I never skipped a class. I was nice to him back then, especially after Mom died.

In grade eleven, I started smoking dope with the same guys I'd hung out with since grade two. The girls liked us because we were doing well in school, and because we were cool and fun to be around and because we smoked dope and listened to Rush. By grade twelve we weren't doing as well in school. We were having a lot of fun but we were always high. Even in class. A couple of the young birds still hung with us but they got tired of the life pretty quickly. A lot of them went to university. Not me. Not Rudy. We smoked up, and watched

TV. Inertia's a fucked up thing. Especially when it involves fucked up habits. My dad called me last night and offered me something that's going to be hard to refuse. I just might get there. George Brown, that is.

But Rudy's always bothering me to get dope. And the registration form doesn't fill itself out.

I'm sweeping up decayed food particles from around the sofa on a Tuesday morning. When I open the door to dump the filth on the tile floor in the hallway, Joseph's sitting in his spot, cradling an Apple iPod. "Hi Ben," he says. He strokes the dials. He delicately stuffs the plastic wrapping into the open box. He sniffs the headphones, and I can't be sure but it looks like he's kissing the iPod itself. "My dad helped me buy it. He gave me half the money for it. I was hoping to get the iPod Hi-Fi, but this is almost as good."

"Really. Your dad sounds like a nice guy."

"He is."

"Can I tell you something, Joseph?"

"What's that?"

"My dad has paid for my tuition at George Brown College. I just have to fill out the registration."

"That's great," says Joseph. "Your dad's a nice guy too."

"Yeah, he is," I say, feeling foolish. I'm in a genuine fucking conversation, which is not something I'm used to.

Joseph's eyes look past me at someone approaching from the elevator.

From behind me Rudy says, "Let me see that, Joseph."

Joseph ignores him, but when Rudy asks again Joseph says, "I haven't even listened to it myself, yet. I haven't downloaded any music."

Rudy motions with his hand and says, "Come on. Give it over."

Joseph reluctantly hands Rudy his iPod.

Rudy puts the headphones on and nods his head to imagined music. "Can I borrow this for a while?" he says.

I drum my dustpan against the railing. "Want to come into the apartment, Rudy? I need to talk to you about something." Rudy turns and when he does, I snatch the iPod and pull the headphones from his ears. I hand them to Joseph and crack the dustpan against the railing.

Joseph runs down the stairs.

"Is there something wrong with you?" Rudy says.

Something is wrong. I can't gut the fucker with a dustpan. I need a knife. Tell you what, God — let's sentence this fucker to purgatory and the boy gets to keep his iPod. Are you with me, Lord? "Yeah, something's wrong, Rudy. I want you to leave Joseph alone. Don't bug him anymore," I say.

"Why do you care about that kid?" Rudy says.

"If you mess with him, I'm going to come back here and have a word with you."

"Come back here?" He laughs. "Come back from where?"

I haven't really thought this through. "I'm going to live with my dad," I say.

"Is that right?" He laughs again. "Just how are you going to toke up at your dad's place?"

"That's not my biggest concern at this point."

"Then get the fuck out before it's dark."

"Tell, you what, Rudy. It won't even take me that long." And it won't. I've got maybe three garbage bags worth of stuff. I'm mindful that I'll have to come back and check on Joseph from time to time. Who knows? Perhaps I'll even renounce weed. Is that really so difficult?

My Horoscope

I DROP MY SUITCASE AND REEBOK DUFFEL bag on the single unruffled bed and massage my creased neck, a result of the twenty-minute walk up Union Avenue, duffel bag banging my hip, shoulder strap gripping the flesh under my ears. A print of Jupiter with its many moons covers one wall. Astrological maps and ancient Greek transcripts are tacked up on the left side of the room. Thick, hardcover books line shelves. The posters and books are immaculately organized. My half of the room is barren.

My new roommate, Cam, is sprawled on the floor. He's tall and soft looking with brown eyes. We met briefly at a get-to-know-you social at Wellington Hall last Thursday. He's studying a weathered zodiac chart. A manual of astrology, *Life According to the Stars*, leans against his leg. He smiles, and asks me when I was born, then consults his chart, and says, "So you're Sagittarius. You don't like to spend too much time in one place, right? Your planets are all in their sixth sector. Oh, but wait a sec — you have a moon in Aquarius, which means that you'll soon be obsessed with something that'll disturb your work, in this case your studies. But don't let me scare you. This chart is usually off. You don't mind if

I use your information in a study I'm doing of every kid at Aberdeen Hall, do you?"

"Not at all," I say. "Where are you from?"

"I'm from Cambridge," he says. "Do you happen to know Julia? I don't know her last name. She's got black, shoulder-length hair. She's from here as well."

"You're going to have to give me more than that," I say.

Cam closes his astrology book, and sits cross-legged, his limbs like spaghetti noodles the way they hang. "She's probably in Aberdeen residence. I met her yesterday in the laundry room."

"I don't know anyone named Julia," I say, laughing, thinking that Cam is obsessed with this girl. It's understandable, but it'll never happen to me.

"I can clean up that stain for you," he says. He's staring at where I've spilled salad dressing on my shirt.

"It's all right. I'll clean it myself later. I need a shower," I say. "Long walk here, right?" I get a bar of Ivory soap from the shaving kit that my father has given me, grab a wrinkled towel stuffed next to my Psych 101 text and walk down the hall to the showers. Cam is following me, lugging a book, which is a concern — I don't want him crowding me. I'd just as soon make a few other friends first.

There is hollering from kids in neighbouring rooms. I'm missing out on something but don't know what. I want to get cleaned up, retrieve the half-full bottle of Bailey's stolen from my parents, and walk down the hallways in the hope that someone will invite me in. Cam is still behind me. A mohawked seven-footer with gentle features dribbles a warped basketball down the hall through wafting incense. In the bathroom, there are about twenty stalls and fifteen sinks. Cam follows me into the shower area in his street clothes. At least he removes his socks and shoes. He corners a red-haired boy, who is lathering himself with soap.

"What are you doing?" the redhead says. "Can't I have my shower in peace?" I give the kid a look and then avert my eyes. I've never actually showered in front of anyone before. Cam lowers himself to the floor by the sinks, the antiseptic tiles scrubbed spotless, though I imagine toothpaste, toilet paper and grime will be everywhere by the second week of school.

The redhead has a dumbstruck expression on his face. "Are you waiting for me?"

"Sorry 'bout that," Cam says. "I'd like to ask you some questions for this study I'm doing. I can ask you later, though."

I'm now in the room of our neighbour, Jim, the redhead. We're listening to Cold Play, sharing my Bailey's. I don't feel like talking because he's got the music turned up and is yelling about how much he hates gays, and how he's going to punch Cam if he approaches him in the shower again. I'm nervous myself, first day on campus and all, but Jim's from Thornhill and I suppose they don't have a lot of gay people there. His room is orderly like Cam's. A kettle spouts steam in the corner, and he offers tea. "Right," I say. "Yeah, know what you mean." Jim and his roommate, a taciturn, gangly guy from Toronto, have turned the two singles into bunk beds. A dark Spiderman duvet cordons off their sleeping area. I lie on the futon sofa, and decide not to challenge his homophobia. The raspberry Pop tart he gives me is three-quarters eaten. I pick three moist crumbs from my lap, toss them in my mouth and stare unabashedly at a picture of a hot high school junior, instantly and righteously envious of this asshole for having such a pretty girlfriend, who in two weeks will probably be down for a visit and will be even cuter than her pic, and I know, for this reason alone, Jim and I will never be close friends.

Cam pokes his head in the room. "I want to clean up that shirt of yours," he says, and I get a queasy feeling.

I tell him not to worry about it, but he insists we go back to our room so he can clean it. I get up, thank Jim for his hospitality, and say for his benefit, "I'm sure as heck not taking off my shirt."

Jim sniggers, a provincial, inconsiderate sound, but Cam just laughs along with us.

Back in our room Cam takes stain remover from his suitcase. I hand over the soiled garment, and lie, half-naked, on my unmade bed. His rigorous scrubbing comforts me. This is a nice experience — someone applying elbow grease in an effort to save one of my collared shirts from the garbage heap. My mother's going to love him.

On our first night the phone rings and wakes me up. Cam gets it and then covers the mouthpiece to explain that it's Laura from Cambridge, and that they've been best friends since grade three. She's married and has moved to Surrey with her husband. He turns the speakerphone on so that I can say hi.

Laura's tone is maturely chipper, older than her twenty-two years. Cam's puffer, is it accessible? Are the other kids nice? Is the art history program going to stimulate him? Is he going to make some nice friends? Tucked under my covers only six feet away, I am in anticipation of her next question. Her voice (to be honest, I haven't paid attention to Cam's responses) activates my lower organ, and I have zero restraint. I gently rub the main artery — need to christen the room, right? — but it takes much longer than normal because violent shaking is out of the question. All done, and one hundred percent feeling shame and panic, because Cam might get a whiff of my coagulating mess. The thought that Cam may have heard me keeps me awake until the fervent rumblings from other rooms cease. Sleep.

Next afternoon we're watching *The Young and the Restless* with some co-eds. Cam is talking to Julia, a brunette with long dark lashes. I signal to him that I don't know her. He asks for her sign and birth date, and then says, "Mars usually stays in whatever zodiac sign it's in for six or seven weeks but in 2009 it will stay in your sign for seven months, which means that you're not going to meet anybody during this period. I mean . . . you're going to have low energy for a while, but I really wouldn't worry about it. I mean, you don't have to believe me, now do you? There are other people who know a lot more about this stuff than I do." Julia rolls her eyes, and moves to where her friends are slumped on the sofa.

She has a pretty, unblemished face but lacks a nice figure. She isn't remarkable at all. She doesn't talk to anyone, except the one really loud girl in the bunch, a tall blonde-haired girl with a ponytail, and even then her comments are nothing more than bland rejoinders to what the loud blonde says. She looks so strait-laced she'd seem out of place in a washroom. Maybe her odourless squeaky-cleanness attracts Cam.

I do my Victor Newman impression — "I think I'll join you in the dining room, darling" — that always makes my little sister laugh, but Julia isn't listening. She's staring at two other freshmen — tree-planters apparently — tucked snugly beside the jabbering ponytail-flopping blonde. These guys are like twins from a rich part of Toronto. They wear their bangs in their eyes, their goatees trimmed, and laugh at each other's jokes. I suddenly feel I'm in danger. I cognitively rule out any evidence that might suggest peril, but the sensation of being in danger is still puzzling and discomfiting. And my Victor Newman impression has failed because the womanizing Victor of the 2003 season has given way to the angry, pill-popping cad at the tail end of 2004.

Cam takes out a moon chart and plots trajectories on a piece of paper on the coffee table. "Gemini. This is a good time for you. You've just come off being sick. Am I right?" he asks the blonde girl with the ponytail.

"I *have* had a cough," she says.

The taller, thinner tree-planter says, "You should take this act to New York."

"I'm wondering if this gets you laid, Cammer," his chubbier counterpart says.

Cam smiles and says, "This isn't a science. It's only a hobby of mine."

He asks me if I want to go back to wash up. We scrub our hands and then join a mass exodus of nervous freshmen heading off to feed. We're soon surrounded by heat lamps and abundant trays of Mugzee's chicken wings and Domino's pizza slices. The grease on the pepperoni trickles, mixing with the bubbling fat from the processed cheese. Cam reads aloud each menu choice, posing pertinent questions to the hair-netted service ladies. I follow him, pretending interest in Caesar salad ingredients, but all the while wondering what we're going to do. The caf is filling up fast on this second day on campus, the first regular day, and I've got to secure a spot at a table, perhaps the biggest move of the year, bigger than deciding my electives, bigger than deciding which university to attend. Cam inadvertently assists me by studying the bean burrito ingredients for toxic additives, buying me time to scope out the cafeteria. I'd love to stand at the foot of the room, in front of the checkout line, and scan the area for a few minutes so I can make the prudent choice, but I'm already too self-conscious. I am self conscious of my self-consciousness. I barely survive, french-fries in hand, by sticking to Cam. He wants to sit with Julia, and I agree, not remembering at first who she is, but lo and behold, she turns out to be the long-lashed, smooth-faced brunette from this afternoon.

Cam sits primly beside her, which leaves me standing behind him, french-fries falling to my feet. She *is* smiling, which puts me at ease. Cam, God bless him, says, "There's a seat, Stewart," which is doubly beneficial. He has *named* me; I have a seat, and am now ensconcing myself between our redheaded neighbour, Jim, who doesn't say hi, and one of the goateed tree-planters from the afternoon. I fit my knees under the table, but my torso can't squeeze in. Neither boy nudges over, but I notice they don't have much room either. The thin half of the tree-planting tandem is histrionically collapsed at the end of the table (one of the girls has just asked if he was taking engineering courses). His forehead is on the table, his goatee collecting flecks of salt. Two gorgeous co-eds are trying to revive him by licking their fingers and sticking them in his ears, which causes movement in my jeans, and which makes me think, so passionately that others must hear, that if only this cretin would right himself and tuck in his elbows, and if everyone shifted slightly, I could thrust my hips forward and *be* physically at the table. My fries, five bites for each salty wedge, distract me. This way I'm not obliged to talk. I'm aching for Cam to make some type of breakthrough with this gang before it's too late, before we descend into the caste of the unnoticed. Each passing hour in this venerable institution is less crucial than the one before it. Cam tells Julia about Laura. "We've been best friends since grade three."

This clearly won't do. I bob my head into the flux, eyes wide with anxiety and say to the long-lashed brunette, "Where are you from, Julia?"

She looks at me for the first time, and I can tell she isn't sure that I've spoken to her, so I repeat the question. She opens her mouth, a pert orifice, and I'm trembling. The slighter of the two goateed guys is telling a story about tree planting, and he wants Julia to listen, so he grabs her arm. "Imagine getting bitten by a dozen skeets on the ass," he says. "Not on the fleshy part of the ass, but right on the, like, sensitive, pink part of the ass, while you're taking care of business, and you've gotta itch and you don't want to get up cause it's gonna get all over you, and you've gotta itch. Did I say that already?" And Julia is now laughing, though I don't know why, because this guy is a moron, a filthy-mouthed moron, but she and the others find him funny, which makes *me* want to be his friend.

"Where on the ass?" I ask. But he's already said where and I'm speaking much too loudly for the intimate space, and he doesn't say anything, which adds to my irrelevance. I feel totally shut out from the group. They all get up and set off to see a documentary on Trudeau at Crosbie Hall, which leaves Cam and me at the table by ourselves. This is okay with me. I go back to the line and get two cheeseburgers and a chocolate mousse.

At bedtime, Cam speaks in a hushed tone. "I wish you'd been there, Laura. I was in the laundry room at my regular time and guess *who* walked in? That's right. The machine across from me. I'm not saying it means anything, but she must have known I'd be there. Put it this way — she didn't go out of her way to do her laundry at a *different* time, right?"

While he's talking, I roll about, both hands rather obviously on my head in a bid to convince him that any past restlessness on my part was just that, restlessness.

"So anyway, Stewart and I ate lunch late because our English class ends at one o'clock on Thursdays," he is saying to Laura. "She ate her lunch and left with some friends and then, I couldn't believe it — she came back ten minutes later to pick up her bag. She stared right at me. Do you think . . . ?"

The Bio 101 text has large, vivid graphs, a large font, and is a more than adequate substitute for class, which is why I'm at the Highbury Market with Cam instead. After buying bananas and strawberries, Cam says he has personal business to attend to. He tries to persuade me to go back to the residence without him but I stick to him. In a pleasant neighbourhood just south of the downtown core, we stop in front of a two-story residence and take in the scenery. I know where he's taken me because I too have looked up the information in the university directory. "This must have been a healthy place to grow up," Cam says. We walk up the driveway, past the detached garage, to a lane. On the other side is a small park.

"A kid would have a great time on that playground equipment," he says.

There are beige curtains in a second-floor window. Is that her bedroom? Did she prance over these two large boulders in the garden? Her mom's garden, perhaps. Did she sit under this willow tree on hot summer days? Did she roll in leaves as a small child? Did she tussle with other girls during games of Red-Rover? Scrape her knees? I can enjoy this voyeuristic indulgence because Cam is here. And he's normal. His presence makes me feel less creepy.

Thank you, Cam.

We stand there for a few more minutes and then leave the neighbourhood and walk back to our dorm.

Nine o'clock. Cam enters our room with a box of brownie mix. I'm lying on my bed, reading *Maxim*.

"Oh — hey Stewart," he says. He bends over, and pulls out a camping stove from under his bed. He cracks an egg, adds water and mix and then stirs the dark sludge. Brownie mix slops on his prized chart and he neglects to wipe it up. I rest the *Maxim* on my chest and say, "Are you going to the library, Cam?"

"No," he says. "I'm going to a friend's."

He leaves the room with the pan resting on his forearm. I know exactly where he's going and feel sick to my stomach, but am relieved when he comes back with a full plate of brownies. He dips his hand into the batch and eats half. He flips the pan on the ground. It's so unlike him to not offer me a piece, but I understand. I slide off the bed and join him on the floor. He has brownie crumbs all over his black turtleneck. Today I'm more civilized than he is. I cut a piece with a knife, and eat it without making a mess. I wish I could assuage his pain, but I can't let him drag me down. In dormitory life, the hurt do not endure. It's the fun loving who get the attention, and so, like any other nineteen-year-old, I leave the room when I hear the first sad crack in his voice. As I close the door I hear him lift the phone.

Cam hasn't come to Psychology class in two days. He's consulted my notes absent-mindedly, not even complaining that they're incomplete. In the cafeteria he has diva status due to his astrological prognostications. I think a little has rubbed off on me. The goateed tree-planters get out of their seats and escort us to their table, where he's treated like a frat brother.

"We've got plans to raise money for cystic fibrosis," says the chubbier twin, bloated from a month of Buck's fried chicken.

"Yeah," says the skinny twin. "You, Cam, will be stationed with the campus radio disc jockeys during homecoming. We've got football players, physics professors and even the university president all lined up to have their charts read."

"I'm not really too much into astrology anymore, guys," Cam says.

There are protestations — Cam's got a gift. Anyone with his talent should take advantage of it. But he isn't interested. "I've got to get more focused on school," he says. He wraps up his salad and leaves the caf.

I put my arm on the thin twin's shoulder and say, "He's gonna do the radio show. Don't worry. He's a little busy, but I'll persuade him to come on board."

I sit down beside Julia but can't think of anything to say.

It's two o'clock on Wednesday afternoon. I'm lying on my bed. I've been sleeping for a few hours. I feel hung-over, though I haven't had anything alcoholic for four days.

A faint scratching noise arouses me to consciousness. Cam is scraping the brownie mix from his chart. He went home for the weekend, and I haven't seen him much since he got back. Jim, the redhead, is in our room, slumped on the floor. Cold Play is blaring from his room, which we can easily hear since he's left both doors open. He's chatting on the Internet, on a site that caters to university students. They've created a hybrid personality, Johnny Aberdeen, a strange combination of Cam's natural modesty and Jim's brashness. Each takes a turn at the keyboard. Whoever isn't typing usually tries to temper the other. Right now Cam's pleading for a more muted response. He's excited because a girl from Fanshawe College has asked Johnny when he was born. Uncharacteristically, Cam shoves Jim out of the way, hunches over the keyboard, and sticks out his elbows, a clear indication that he's taken over. I engage my mind temporarily to imagine what he might be saying to this girl from Fanshawe.

Jim is laughing at what Cam has written. "You aren't going to try to meet her, are you?"

"You better believe it," says Cam.

I lean over so I'm facing them. "Hey, Cam. You haven't consulted my horoscope in a while."

"Just a sec."

He turns his back to briefly examine his chart. When I ask him again what's in store for me, he shrugs and goes back to the keyboard. I'm happy that he has friends, that he's managed to pull himself out of the doldrums, but everything hasn't been so easy for me. You see, Julia hasn't called me back. I left three messages with her roommate last week. I can't study. My body odor is pungent. My face has broken out in acne. I sleep two hours every night and when I'm awake I'm deeply anxious. Oh God, I can't even . . . .

The Lover

I GET OUT OF MY '98 PONTIAC and walk up the dusty driveway to the front porch, where three of the Riverdale Group Home members sit, smoking hand-rolled, unfiltered cigarettes around a tiny pot of sand and butt ends. When they see my six-foot-six-inch frame bending to greet them, their eyes brighten. "Can we have macaroni and cheese for lunch, Mark?" says Jeremy, rising from his plastic lawn chair.

"Anything you want." What a picture — me with hyper-manic, sunken eyes and distended nose, against Jeremy's sedated, bloated, ruddy face and still eyes, the result of years of chlorpromazine.

In the living room I reach under the flap at the bottom of the sofa and pick up the kitten, which squirms in my arms. I rub the kitten's belly, and place my nose on its forehead. "Hey, little kitty. You like to be rubbed, right?" The kitten hisses, and swipes. Scratch marks, like miniature red train tracks, appear on my wrist. "That hurt, cat," I say. The kitten falls, and scampers from the room. I dab the cut with a napkin.

In the bright, fly-infested kitchen Vivian, shaking her bangs out of her eyes, is swinging a wing-stained swatter, zombie like, at fat, intrepid flies. Jeremy is grating the cheese.

He's cleanly shaven, his hair greased back, and is wearing an ironed, pale-blue dress shirt with nice-fitting, beige slacks. He hovers over a block of cheddar, pressing the cheese against the grater, then scoops cheese into his hand and dumps it in the casserole dish.

"Maybe you should wash your hands," I say.

He says, "Yeah, of course."

Down the hall Sidney is grasping the belt of his trousers — if not they'd drop to his ankles. There's a bulge in his back pocket I hope isn't a turd. Sid walks up the inclining floor. Contractors have poured cement under the house to secure the unstable foundation, but the incline won't be repaired. We use any extra money we have for our daily trip to Tim Horton's.

Jeremy says, "Do you know what I liked about the last time we made macaroni, Mark? I liked the crackers that we mixed in. Do you think we can do that again?"

I stick my head into the common room, where Sidney is now on the soiled sofa, his legs tucked under him, eyes docilely intent on the wall beside the TV, undistracted by Alex Trebek and *Jeopardy*. He smiles a broad, Grinch-like smile that accentuates every wrinkle on his puckish face. "CJBK Mark, CJBK."

"Any of you guys want to go to Shoppers with me to get some crackers?" I say. "Jeremy wants some in the macaroni and cheese."

I push the small cart down the aisle. Jeremy, Sidney and Vivian, the only female member of the group home, trail me. Sidney's shoelace tangles in the bottom of the cart. He kicks at the wheel with the back of his heel and falls to one knee.

Jeremy huffs, pushes Sidney to the side and upends the cart. He kneels and tries to untangle Sid's shoelace.

"Oh-oh, Mark. Can't get out," says Sid, curling up skittishly on the polished floor.

I focus on the lovely cashier behind the counter. She removes a napkin from her pocket and delicately pats her lips. Her friend from the other till joins her and the two of them sit on stools and chat in a breezy manner. The girl with the napkin pouts. She plays with the elastic band that holds her blonde hair in place. Her left calf rests gently on a third stool.

Jeremy rights the cart, which then tips unsteadily and almost crashes again. He grabs the cracker box that lies in the middle of the aisle and slams it into the cart.

God she looks lovely. Look at her fingers. They're so tiny. She handles the cracker box so delicately. I love how her nose turns up. I'd love to stick my nose in her armpit. What does she do in her free time? Mmmm . . . She loves drinking coffee with her girlfriends. She loves movies. She is snotty to her mother but in a cute way. Oh no, she's looking my way. I want to get away from her so I can think about her some more. Oh Jesus.

"That'll be three dollars and fifty-five cents."

I give her the money. "We had some problems with our cart."

"They are kind of old," she says. "Have a nice evening."

The noodles and cheese from lunch have hardened on the unwashed plates that we've set to the side of the dining room table to make room for our card game. Vivian's watermelon-sized head sways. She threatens to completely lose her balance, crash from her chair, writhe on the floor, and cry for her mother, the same person who callously left her at the home two years ago, never to visit, not even once. Vivian's hands shake. Jeremy articulates what I'm thinking. "You've got to play some time, Vivian." She lays down a queen of hearts. The card totters on the edge of the table. With his stubby middle finger, Jeremy drags the queen so that it's beside the deck. "Always, always place your card in the middle of the table," he says. He lays the ace on her queen. "That's euchre last time I checked." I look at the leftover bauer in my hand, which is useless now that Viv and I have been euchred. Careless playing on my part, I think, but *what time's the cashier off work?*

Jeremy sticks his hand into the box of crackers, gropes around, and then plucks out three, dropping them on the table. "These crackers have worms in them," he says.

Sidney leans on the table. "They do? Oh-oh. Alex Trebek, Mark."

I shove one in my mouth. "I don't think they'd let worms get into the mix."

"Who wouldn't?" Jeremy says.

I turn the box so I can read the label. "I don't know, but they don't put worms in their crackers, Jeremy. You've got to take my word for it."

Jeremy takes out his Swiss army knife, pulls out a blade and hacks at one of the crackers. He picks up a piece and examines it carefully. He says, "Looks just like the skin of a worm."

"Tell you what, Jeremy," I say. "If you want, we can go back to Shoppers and get our money back. It could be fun. What do you think?"

"I don't know if we have to go back there, Mark."

"No, no. It's settled. Let's get back our money. Get in the van, guys."

I smile at the lovely cashier. "We're back. I don't mean to trouble you, but we opened the crackers back at the home and we — one of the members, Jeremy, here . . . " I point at Jeremy, who looks justifiably upset, "claims that there are worms in the crackers we just bought."

She takes a cracker from the box, gives it a cursory examination, and says, "It's just the way they bake them. What do you want me to do? I can give you a refund on the product if you think it's damaged."

"I guess that would be okay, if you don't mind."

She prices the box again and then punches her till. She hands me three dollars and fifty-five cents and says, "Here you go."

"No problem." I pause and say, "I'm a worker at the group home, you know."

"What do you mean?"

"I'm not a member."

"I see."

"Do you want to come to a Hallowe'en party at the house next Wednesday? Hallowe'en's not until the following Saturday so it won't disrupt any of your trick or treating, heh-heh."

"I work until eight o'clock that night. I don't know. We'll see."

"Perfect." I give her my Riverdale Group Home card and say, "The party starts at eight o'clock."

In the car ride back to the house I turn to Jeremy, who is sitting beside me in the front seat. "I love that cashier."

Jeremy says, "Does she love you too, Mark?"

"I think she does. I've put in a lot of work. I've been going to that place for five months."

Jeremy's costume design skills are impressive. He cuts up an old, grey shirt. He paints a pattern on a bicycle helmet that cracked the year before. He scours the house for materials, finds an old tire rim and then throws it out because it won't do.

I say, "You don't have to spend so much time on my costume."

Jeremy smiles. "It's nothing," he says. He's lying on the carpet in his austere bedroom, tying together plastic milk containers painted black — so they'll fit around me, I guess, as armour. His moist breath fogs his thick glasses. He grabs the tails of his Pierre Cardin dress shirt, his belly popping loose, takes off and licks the lenses, then wipes them. He pitches the glue bottle at his clothes hamper. His thick fingers nimbly smooth tinfoil over the cardboard shield. His thumb barely squeezing the scissors, he cuts Vivian's stockings and then sews them to the chain mail. At last I see his genius. I'm going to be a medieval knight. How can Jeremy, a paranoid schizophrenic with patricidal fantasies, be so inept and yet so creative?

I avoid the main street and creep down the back alley. I drop the sword and some of the tinfoil scrapes off, exposing dull plastic. I curse and slide it back under my belt. There's a run in my nylons and I curse again. Outside the store a homeless man with a sunburned face says, "Can you spare any change, Governor?"

"Sorry. I don't have any pockets."

I stick my head through the sliding glass doors and am relieved to see the cashier at her till. My grey helmet bobs up the aisle. Given my lanky frame I am, of course, visible to everyone as I emerge from behind a rack of potato chips and saunter up to her.

"Oh, hi," she says. "Look, I have customers."

"It's okay." I wave my hand to show her she has nothing to worry about. "I just came here to remind you about the party."

"Thanks," she says.

"I hope to see you later. You still have the card, right?"

She nods without looking at me. I pretend for a minute that the chain mail limits my freedom of movement and then I leave.

"I don't know if the chicken wings are ready to come out of the oven," Jeremy says.

I say, "What?"

"The chicken wings."

It's late in the evening and I'm tired. "Yes, let's get them out of the oven." I grab the pan and then jump back, swearing. I rinse my blistered fingers under cold water, then go to my office to rest for a while. When I come out Vivian is wiping the counter with a dishcloth.

"How could she not show up?" I ask her. "She said she'd come. I hate it when people don't do what they say they're going to do. Why couldn't she come for, say, fifteen minutes? It was a good party."

"Who didn't come to the party?" Vivian says.

"The cashier at Shoppers."

"Which one?" she says.

"The pretty one. Blonde hair."

"She isn't pretty!" Vivian whips her dirty apron off and throws it on the ground. She waves a bottle of Pledge dangerously close to my eyes.

"I don't care. Blind me for all I care."

Ten years pass. My hairline has receded, and I've shaved off my moustache. In the middle of a heat wave, a young woman volunteer, licking a cherry Popsicle, walks into our sloping hallway. She has a freckled face, narrow eyes, and long smooth legs which start at her tight Adidas shorts. She looks at Jeremy, who, with his trimmed sideburns, creaseless Khaki shorts and sports sandals, probably gives her the impression that he's the staff member on duty. She looks confused when Jeremy says, "Mark told us you might take us to Tim Horton's. They've got double-chocolate doughnuts for forty cents."

"Maybe," the volunteer says. "I'm only here for an hour today. If Mark wants me to go, I'll go."

"Mark Zile," I say, and offer her my hand.

She turns to me and says, "Hi, I'm Shirley. Zile — that's a Latvian name, isn't it?"

I beam. "Yes it is. How did you know that?"

"My sister had a friend who was Latvian," Shirley says, "and we went to the Latvian Community Centre with her as kids."

"Is that right? I was probably there too. We went every week. At the time I didn't like it but I look back fondly on that period."

"I was always curious," she says. "I grew up feeling like I didn't have any ethnic identity and was always very curious about European culture."

"Well, if you grew up with Latvians, you know what we're like." I take her hand, in a chivalrous gesture, and lift it gallantly to my lips and kiss it.

She giggles. "Can I have my hand back?" She then says, "Would you like me to take the guys to Tim Horton's?"

I rummage through a cupboard. Cookies found, I arrange them in a pyramid on a plate, and then carry them into the dining room. There's definitely an invigorated bounce in my step. "Here you go, miss," I say, affecting a Latvian accent. Vivian looks up at me appreciatively. "Thanks Mark," she says. Her anti-psychotic meds bloat her tongue and slacken the muscles in her throat so her speech is muffled.

Jeremy looks at Sidney and says, "What about us?"

I ignore him and hide behind the living room curtains, looking for Shirley's car. She's promised to help Vivian bake a rhubarb pie. I can assist them with that.

When Shirley arrives, I meet her in the hallway. "Glad you could come back to our home, miss. How do you say, 'Welcome,' in Latvian?"

"I've no idea," she says, shaking her head, and bounds up the stairs to see Jeremy.

An hour later I shuffle sheepishly into Jeremy's room with a mug of tea for her. "Nice to see you again, miss." I reach to touch her hand but she withdraws it.

"I just had a fight with my housemate, Mark," she says. "Jeremy's been a great listener. Haven't you, Jeremy?"

"Yeah, I suppose." says Jeremy. "Always lay your card on the one played before it." Jeremy takes the mug and sets it on the floor. "I don't like it when anything else is on the table. Nothing but the cards." He sucks in a breath through his teeth. "Mark and me beat Bob Coolidge and Dean at Tim Horton's on Thursday."

"I'm sorry to have unloaded all of my problems on you, Jeremy." She looks at me. "I have to go."

"It's okay," Jeremy says. "I know how you feel, Shirley."

She puts on her sandals and steps into the hallway.

I say, "Miss. Miss." I run after her into the hall. Out of anxiety I betray my Canadian accent and say, "Hold on a second. As you know, miss, when a beautiful lady leaves a house, a Latvian man must see her out the door. It's my duty to wish you a fine week and for me to say . . . "

"Yes, I'll see you later, Mark. Have a nice weekend. See you Jeremy."

"Call me later if you want, Shirley," says Jeremy.

Weeks pass. I wait doggedly at the bay window. Isn't persistence rewarded?

Then, a tug at my shirt. Jeremy's face is animated. "Shirley called me, Mark. She said she didn't feel like doing volunteer work anymore. She said that I could call her anytime if I wanted."

Sid and I are in the kitchen. I bend over and pour milk into the bowl. I feed the obese cat and pet his white fur. He doesn't return my affection.

Sidney says, "My sister's cat . . . fat cat, Mark. My sister loves me, Mark."

"Is your sister married?"

"Yes. I don't know. CJBK Radio, Mark."

"Sidney invited me here," says Adriana, Sidney's sister. "Do you mind if I ask — I don't mean to embarrass you — but Sidney told me you wanted to meet me. Is that true?"

"Well, it's always nice to meet new people."

"Yeah, at my age I should take some risks. If I don't make any effort I might as well throw in the towel," she says, laughing.

"I know. Being single in your early forties is challenging. I love being here with the guys. These guys are like family for me — though like you I'd love to meet someone as well."

She says, "I had this boyfriend once . . . "

Jeremy, Adriana, Vivian and I sit in front of the cold fireplace. Adriana rolls the dice, cheers whimsically when she lands on pink, and says, "Humphrey Bogart in Casablanca." This board game's consuming her, I think.

Sid doesn't pay much attention to his sister even though she's his one advocate. Last year he told Adriana on the phone that he needed to get away from Jeremy, who'd been bugging him constantly about picking up his pee-stained Fruit of the Looms. She called my boss and demanded that someone find Sid a new room.

Why doesn't she notice me? If only I could somehow summon You, God, and have You force her to see me from Vivian's point of view. Vivian loves my sense of humour. She knows that I'm a caring person. I smile at Adriana when I pick up the dice, but she impatiently implores me to roll. She gives me a clue after I land on orange, and gently mocks me when I bungle this easy sports question. I stare unblinkingly at her even though it's no longer my turn, or hers. After a while she glares back.

Jeremy rolls, and lands on orange. He says, "I don't have a clue as to what the correct answer might be."

"It's fishing or angling," Adriana says.

"You're not so smart!" Vivian says. She's been seething for a while and I probably should've done something to prevent this outburst.

"Be nice to her, Viv," I say.

"Vivian should be more polite to Adriana," Jeremy says. "She's our guest."

"Be polite to my sister, Vivian. Be polite to my sister, Vivian," says Sidney.

Vivian slaps Sidney's mouth. One of the game pieces nestled between his lips goes flying. A thin gob of spit hangs from his chin, which he wipes with his shoulder.

"I have to go anyway," says Adriana.

"Hold on," I say. "I'm going snowboarding this weekend. I have my own skis. I wasn't sure that I had the money for the boots, but my dad persuaded me to put it on my Visa. I love that man. I can't see myself living anywhere but at home, except of course if I get married, but that's not something I think too much about. I guess what I'm trying to say is that I just love to snowboard. I didn't fall too often the first time, but all it takes is one wipe-out. I bruised my thigh. Do you want to see my leg?" I roll up my pants but can't get them past my knee. "Oh well, I'll show it to you some other time — it's big and purple . . . "

Sidney and Jeremy are searching for the missing game piece. I stand near the curtain and watch Adriana's car roll down the driveway. *If I don't get to her right away she's going to find another boyfriend. I'm going to be left with these people. I will die with these people. If I don't end up with her, I'll be alone, except I'll be one of them. No more worker-member relationship. If I can't be with her I'm going to check into here, live out my life in drudgery, doing the dishes, going to Tim Horton's, and watching television. Maybe I'll marry Viv. At least I've got an option. After she's had her meds she can carry on a decent enough conversation. Fuck. Fuck. I've gotta get to Adriana right now!*

Left hand clutching his trousers, Sidney says, "Don't call her, Mark. CJBK Mark. Rolling with the tunes, Mark. Don't call her, okay Mark?"

Lifetimes later the wallpaper has peeled in the corners. In the barren living room Vivian asks me if we can go to Tim Horton's.

"We're helping Jeremy right now, Viv."

"Oh, right," says Vivian. She trudges off to the kitchen.

Jeremy takes down the prints of Lake Louise in his room, then removes the clothing I've packed in his suitcase, and meticulously refolds his underwear and T-shirts. With a long poster of the New York skyline wrapped around his hips, Sid says, "Is this okay, Jeremy? Is this okay?"

Panicked, Jeremy runs to where Sidney's standing. "You've got to gently roll up the posters." He seizes it from Sid and rolls it up, and then turns to me, sucking air noisily through his lips, and says, "I'm going to like doing things my own way for a while. Sidney can't get in my way over there."

"Sure thing, Jeremy," I say. "But who are you going to talk with? You're going to miss Sid and Vivian, aren't you?"

"I won't miss anyone," he says.

On the way we stop at a mall where a nearly self-sufficient Jeremy enters the Future Shop, and speaks to a teenaged clerk. "I'd like a Panasonic 500, young man," he says. "I'm going to pay cash." He peels 300 dollars from his wallet and hands it over. I make a detour past Young Thai and pick up two plates of green coconut curry wrapped in foil. At Jeremy's new apartment on Mills Street we unpack his sparse belongings and eat in the uncluttered one-room, smoking until midnight. Sitting with this man I've known for over fifteen years, I feel that we're sharing a special moment. Jeremy reveals that the empty room intimidates him. Smoke swirling in the dark room adds to the eerie quiet. I think about the dullness of our existence at the group home. I'm about to leave when Jeremy grabs me. "I need you to visit me, Mark. I need this more than anything."

I visit him Tuesday evening and am shocked: his normally nicely trimmed moustache has grown unwieldy, and there's a lopsided quality to his face. He's walking around without a shirt on, and I can smell his body odour. With help from Sidney we move a second-hand, beige sofa into the apartment. I bring in a night table and curtains. Jeremy, puffing madly on a cigarette, paces the room while I hook up the cable.

"Do you want to play euchre, Jeremy?" I say.

"I don't really care much for euchre, thank you very much," Jeremy says gravely. "The TV's okay Mark, but I really need you to visit."

I'm tying Vivian's shoelace. Her lack of balance is an effect of the tiny purple pill, chlomopromazine, which causes her to stumble even when her footing is secure. "Just be a second, Viv. I've almost got it."

Through her legs I see someone who is obviously not a member. She's wearing an ironed and elegant-looking yellow blouse. There's a waft of Chanel perfume. Is she the new worker that I'm to train today?

Viv's shoelace is properly tied. My hands are still on her swollen ankles, my tongue semi-protruding. A flush of dopamine burps through my cerebral cortex: *I must look like a pervert. Woe big fella, there are many plausible explanations as to why I'm on my hands and knees in front of Vivian: maybe she's twisted her knee and I'm tending to it, or maybe she fell down and I'm feeling for bruises. There's no reason for this woman to think I'm a pervert. Maybe I was just doing something as harmless as tying her shoes.*

The new worker's struggling to get her spring jacket off over her bony elbows. She's probably disoriented herself. With a gentle push I get away from Vivian, unpleasant thoughts floating away with the ebbing dopamine. The woman walks toward me, her right leg muscled, and her left dragging. Wait a second! What is this? A bum wheel? One of God's imperfections? She keeps her balance by hyper-extending her ankle so her heel presses against the floor, giving her leverage and steadying her. This is actually quite liberating for me. Not that I rejoice in her misfortune. Rather, I'm simply more comfortable around other people, who like me, have a physical disability. Is this really so awful? I remind myself that, despite any impulse, I must not bring up her chicken leg. "Hi. We were expecting you," I say. "I'm Mark."

"I'm Nicole. Nice to meet you, Mark. Who is this?" she says to Vivian.

"What's wrong with your leg?" Vivian says. She sort of laughs, but the noise could be confused with a smoker's cough.

"I was born with this. What's your name, dear?"

"Vivian."

"I didn't notice it," I say. I smile at her.

"I think it looks funny!" says Vivian.

"Viv, maybe you should show Nicole where the office is so that she can put her bag down if she wants." *Dear Lord, if you can hear me now, I want to tell you that I've noticed this woman's atrophied, hideously deformed leg, and, I'll level with you, Lord, it doesn't bug me one bit. I will even gently gnaw on the purple limb to show you that I'm telling the truth. The only thing is this, Lord — let her accept my scoliosis. The curvature of my spine is even more pronounced these days. She can't find my bald head unattractive either. Have we got a deal, Lord?*

The cat lying on the sofa yawns and slowly gets up on its feet. Now sixteen years old, it sidles up to me and rubs its belly against my leg. "How are you, Felix?" I say. "You want a nice belly scratch, don't you?"

Nicole is studying me. I pick some lint from my sweater and smooth the wrinkles on it above my belt buckle. "We have a great group of people here," I say. "I think you're really going to like it."

"I can see that," she says, "but I'm a little nervous. I got my degree from George Brown just last year but nobody's hiring. I don't want to mess up this opportunity." Her grey hair is tied back in a ponytail that flicks from left to right off her wiry shoulders.

"You're going to be fine."

So what if I am self-conscious of my scoliosis and baldpate. I want to show off how much I know about the Riverdale Group Home: how dispensing medicine is crucial to the mental health of each member, how it's important not to condescend to them but to treat them with dignity. How Sidney is agitated when anyone is in the hallway outside his room while he's putting on his pajamas, how Vivian doesn't like to be asked how she's doing, how John and Sidney can't sit beside each other at the dinner table because Sid thinks that John is always making fun of him.

"Come with me," I say, and we enter the washroom, where Sidney is standing in the tub, scrubbing mold from the tiles. He trembles at the sight of the new worker. I introduce them, get down on my knees and help him clean the wall. "CJBK Radio, Mark. Rolling with the tunes, Mark."

Bending into the tub, Nicole pats Sid's lower back, and he makes a just-audible purring noise. Sid is my litmus test for anyone new to Riverdale. I have a nascent erection — one that I attribute to pleasant thoughts in general, and not from any excitement generated from watching her touch Sidney. At least I pray that this is the case.

"I cleaned the bathrooms at my placement at Hillcrest," Nicole says.

I think: what if *she* is trying to impress *me*? An equally foreign thought: Do *I* like *her*?

In the kitchen Vivian is writing out a grocery list. "We might need some more mayonnaise," I say, "and we'll probably need another two loaves of bread."

Nicole says, "I really like the scarf that you're wearing, Vivian," which is nice, but a lie. Viv's scarf is tattered, and a muddy-brown colour, as if Viv has cleaned herself with it. "Ss-stay away from my ss-scarf . . . " Vivian's voice trails off. She shuffles away, her head down, greasy bangs drooping over her flushed face.

How delightful it is to work with someone like Nicole. I make a new pact with God. I don't actually need to be her boyfriend if we can be friends. If we can work in a pleasant environment together, she may stick around long enough to appreciate my strengths. Perhaps I should conceal my longing. After all, there's no pressing need for her to consider me a suitor. "You have a warm touch with the members," I say. I'm again astonished. Nicole is blushing, not necessarily because she fancies me, of course, but because I appreciate her for *her* strengths.

To my relief, Sidney comes out of his room to show me a large perspiration stain on his shirt. The pleasant exchange between Nicole and me has been almost too much. I hustle Sid back to his room and raid his closet. Then, wearing jeans and clean shirt, Sidney bounds out to the patio where Nicole is smoking with Vivian. I follow in time to see Viv flick ashes on Nicole's arm.

"She's not an ashtray, Vivian," I say.

John brings out a malformed cake, fingerprints on the icing's surface. I attack it with my fork, taking a big piece, patting my stomach. "I've gotta keep feeding this thing."

Finding myself alone with Nicole, the sun setting behind the house, I coolly say, "Our house is a gang. We're all just looking to get along. Sometimes I think I'm the one who is mentally afflicted."

Nicole giggles unnaturally, a shrill noise from her thin lips.

Oh Lord, I can't do this. What makes me think I can pull this off? Let's examine my history with women, shall we? What do I see? The nervous, deranged twenty-four-year-old, the thirty-three-year-old insufferable liar, and the needy, desperate twit of my forties.

But is it too late?! I can still get my act together. I can feel it. Euphoria! Why didn't I feel this before? Forget about before.

A week later in the garden I ask, "Are you single?"

"Yes."

I'm alone with her for the first time that day. The members are inside washing up. I walk with her from the shed to the house. I listen to her anecdotes about high school — she always felt self-conscious because of her autistic sister, and lived with guilt because she hadn't given her enough support at school, and hadn't really taken care of her.

How life affirming it is to listen to someone. I recognize the look on her face. Her expression — the anxious one — is exactly my own. I understand that she's vulnerable too. I am full of love. I want to comfort this anxiety-laden woman, and for the first time, I follow an instinct that proves healthy. I pull her to some shrubbery and kiss her on the lips.

Jeremy's boss at Value Mart calls and tells me that Jeremy hasn't been to work for three days. On the phone, Jeremy's voice sounds frail. I enter with the key he's given me. He is lying on the sofa, unshaven, his soiled collar tucked the wrong way, and his glasses crooked. The nine of diamonds and the seven of spades are on his chest. I take his large, burly hand — a hand that never shook, but now does — and lead him from the vomit-smelling apartment and into the van. Jeremy glumly returns to Riverdale and is treated as if he never left.

A month later he is finishing a grilled cheese sandwich when he has a massive heart attack.

Sidney and John wear musty suits rooted out of a closet in the unused downstairs hallway. The men are mirthlessly disinterested in the proceedings, that is until Shirley rolls in. They slowly come to their feet and, heads down, walk over to her. She's wearing the frumpy blouse that she wore when she first volunteered at the home all those years ago. Her uneasy behaviour makes me think that she's ready to make a quick exit.

"Nice to see you," I say.

"He was calling me two or three times a day," she says, gently crying.

"You were really nice to him, Shirley," I say. I put my hand on her arm. She's nervous, but I keep it there anyway. "You were great to him," I repeat and look into her eyes.

"Thanks," she mumbles. "He was such a gentle guy." She then says, "How about you? You've changed."

My woman is bringing me lemonade. I pat her on the bum and say, "This is bliss." Viv and Sid are snug on both sides of me. We're all lounging under an umbrella. I'm still at Riverdale. Nicole, though, works at a different group home. It just made sense to us for her to find another job. After all, we're hitched. Sex with Nicole is wild! Her atrophied leg doesn't even get in the way much. We did it once in the common room when the guys were asleep. I think Vivian was watching, which is a little scary, but Nicole doesn't need to know. At times she can be a little possessive, but who am I to complain? At fifty-two she's too old to give me babies, but we've adopted, kind of. Viv's cooking is getting better. Sid isn't as nervous. He hasn't shit himself in three years. And I like to think about Jeremy on a nice day like this.

Are You taking care of him?

DEREK HAYES has worked as a high school teacher in Toronto, Taipei, and Istanbul. His stories have appeared in literary journals such as *The Fiddlehead* and *The Dalhousie Review*. He was born in London, Ontario and lives in Toronto.